PADDLE STEAMERS

An Illustrated History
of Steamboats
on the Mississippi
and its Tributaries

KEN WATSON

W · W · NORTON & COMPANY

New York   *London*

Published simultaneously in Canada by Stoddart Publishing
Printed in the United States of America.
The text of this book is composed in ITC Bookman Light, with
display type set in Trocadero. Composition by PennSet, Inc.
Manufacturing by The Murray Printing Company
Book designed by Jacques Chazaud

First Edition

Library of Congress Cataloging in Publication Data
Watson, Ken.
   Paddle steamers.
   1. Paddle steamers—United States—History.
I. Title.
VM461.W38   1984   386'.22436'0973   83–21977

ISBN 0-393-01865-2

W. W. Norton & Company, Inc., 500 Fifth Avenue, New York, N.Y. 10110
W. W. Norton & Company Ltd., 37 Great Russell Street, London WC1B 3NU

1 2 3 4 5 6 7 8 9 0

CONTENTS

Acknowledgments

My interest in the American paddlesteamer began with the construction of an eighteen-foot-long working model of the sternwheeler "Idlewild". In pursuit of knowledge of the subject I became aware of the lack of published information available in Britain on the American riverboats. A journey to America helped fill the gaps in this knowledge. In the process, many new friends were made. Time, material and knowledge were unselfishly given by them, and introductions to many other enthusiasts followed. The object of this book is to introduce the public to a page of American river history, with thanks to those friendly steamboat buffs whose assistance made it all possible: Rita and Alan Bates of Louisville; Sue and Dana Eastman of Alton, St. Louis; Claire and Gene Fitch of the paddleboat "Claire E"; Sally and Bob Lumpp of Hannibal; Bill Reynolds and Campus Martius of Marietta; and Bill Berkman (now deceased) of the U.S. Corps of Engineers. My appreciation also goes to Yeatman Anderson III, Curator of Rare Books and Special Collections of the Public Library of Cincinnati and Hamilton County, who selected some of the many photographs used in this book. My grateful thanks go to the S & D *Reflector*, the magazine of the sons and daughters of the pioneer rivermen, who are dedicated to preserving the memory of the American paddlesteamer.

I would like to record my thanks to the organizations and companies mentioned below, who supplied photographs and details on paddle steamers. A special thank you goes to the companies still in the business for photographs of the many paddle steamers still threshing their way along the American Rivers.

American Waterways Operators Inc., 1600 Wilson Boulevard, Suite 1101 Arlington, Virginia. 22209.

Belle of Louisville Operating Board, Riverfront Plaza, Foot of Fourth Street, Louisville, Kentucky, 40202.

Delta Queen Steamboat Company, 511 Main Street, Cincinnati, Ohio, 45202.

Department of the Army, Louisville District, Corps of Engineers, P.O. Box 59, Louisville, Kentucky, 40201.

Lake George Steamboat Company, Steel Pier, Lake George, New York, 12845.

Missouri Historical Society, Jefferson Memorial Building, Forest Park, St. Louis, Missouri, 63112.

New Orleans Steamboat Company, 2340 International Trade Mart,
New Orleans, Louisiana, 70130.

Ohio Historical Society Inc., Ohio River Museum, Marietta,
Ohio, 45750.

Ohio River Museum, Marietta, Ohio, 45750.

Public Library of Cincinnati & Hamilton County, 800 Vine Street,
Cincinnati, Ohio, 45202.

Rock Hill Steamboats, P.O. Box 4012, Louisville, Kentucky, 40204.

River Entertainment Inc., 230 East Ontario Place, Suite 1004,
Chicago, Illinois, 60611.

Sons and Daughters of Pioneer Rivermen, publishers of
the S & D Reflector.

Southern Comfort Corporation, 1220 North Price Road, St. Louis,
Missouri, 63132.

A Note on Illustrations

The illustrations in this book were selected in an attempt to make the reader aware of the wide variety of boats under the general category of paddle steamer. It should also be noted that many paddle steamers had the same names. Some were different boats under individual ownership, but more frequently a steamboat company carried the name through a succession of steamers.

The drawings used in this book are by J. V. Piper, and many were based on original sketches published in *The Western Rivers Steamboat Cyclopedium.* They have been reproduced here by kind permission of the author, Lawrence Bates.

MISSOURI R.

YELLOWSTONE R.

LITTLE MISSOURI R.

CANNONBALL R.

MISSOURI R.

MOREAU R.

CHEYENNE R.

WHITE R.

JAMES R.

MINNESO...

NIOBRARA R.

PLATTE R.

REPUBLICAN R.

SALMON R.

SMOKEY HILL R.

KANSAS R.

ARKANSAS R.

CIMARRON R.

N. CANADIAN R.

S. CANADIAN R.

RE...

| 0 | 100 | 200 | 300 | 400 | 500 MILES |

CHAZAUD

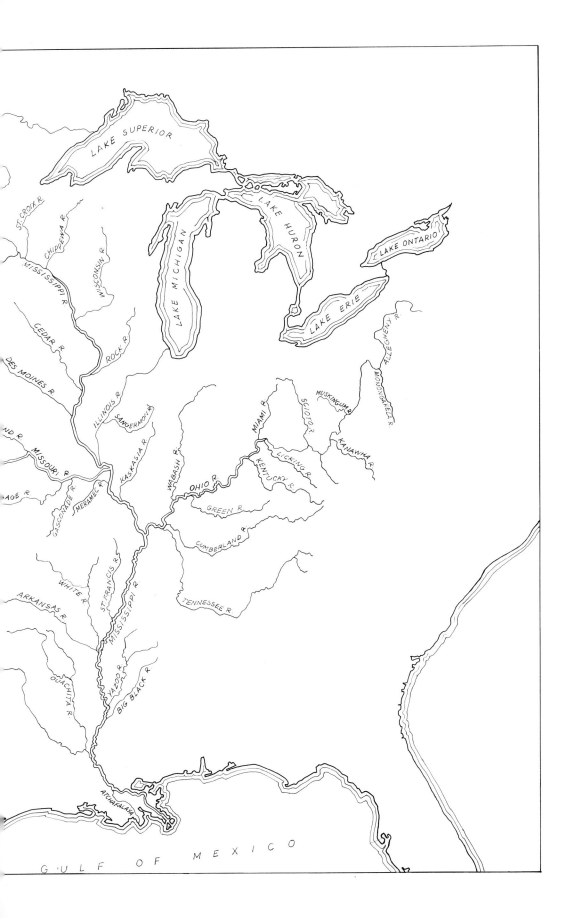

1

PIROGUES TO PUSHBOATS

In America at the end of the eighteenth century, overland transport lagged far behind that of the open sea. The roads were poor, the costs of carriage high, and the journeys long and slow. Except to serve local needs, highway transport played a minor role in commercial intercourse. Rivers comprised the principal inland waterways, but in contrast to the sea, the conditions of rivers prevented navigation by use of sails on most waterways except in a minor way. Our story concerns those rivers which empty into the Mississippi—there are over fifty in number, from the minor tributaries to such large rivers as the Missouri and Ohio, and they contain an estimated 16,000 miles of navigable waters. Along those miles many thousands of riverboats made their way—boats embracing many different designs, all fulfilling their diverse needs. In light of the vast and varied world of riverboats observations can be only of a general nature.

Riverboat men, by their very calling were of an independent nature,

The Red River expedition.

Our location for this story is the Mississippi Valley. It's extreme length from north to south is almost twenty-five hundred miles, with a maximum descent of more than sixteen hundred feet. Three quarters of this drop is in the upper half of the valley. The Mississippi river rises in Lake Itasca in northern Minnesota, flowing generally in a southerly direction, and serves as a boundary for the States of Minnesota, Wisconsin, Iowa, Illinois, Missouri, Kentucky, Tennessee, Arkansas, Mississippi and Louisiana in it's 2,470 mile course into the Gulf of Mexico. Our time for this journey begins in the early 1800s and brings us up to the present day.

Indian pirogues, dugout canoes, were possibly the first craft to move cargoes on the rivers. These craft were used well into the 1800s. The next was the keelboat, and along with this the flatboat appeared. The flatboat, or barge, was used for hauling freight and passengers during the great westward migration. It was during this period, around 1812, that the steamboat was born. It eclipsed the keelboat service down to New Orleans by reducing transit time from months to a week, weather permitting, and reached its peak around 1860. But by the end of the century the steamboat was virtually extinct. Railroads had halved transit time, regardless of the weather. Eventually large riverborne towing fleets regained most of the bulk cargo traffic by reducing the cost per ton well below any figure that the railroads could quote.

often as not going their own sweet way without notice of each other. Many tales were told among them, often embellished to suit the audience, and truths were lost in interpretation. With that in mind, the reader will understand the contradictions in the history of the revolution on the rivers which took place during the 1800s.

The pirogue (a hollowed out log) was the Mississippi version of the Ohio River's dugout canoe.

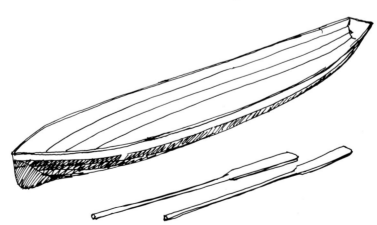

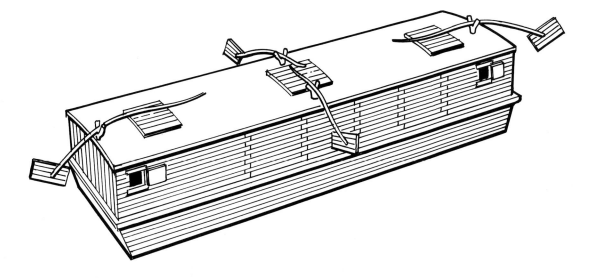

The flatboat or broadhorn.

Flatboats and keelboats gave the river its earliest commerce. They floated and sailed from the upper rivers down to New Orleans. Those intending to return changed their cargoes there, and were then tediously warped and poled back by hand. The round trip could take up to nine months. The flatboat was not so much a boat as a great clumsy box, which any carpenter, handyman, or farmer could knock together out of rough lumber. It was a rectangular boxlike structure with sides about five feet high, and varied in length from twenty to sixty feet, the width between ten and twenty-five feet. These unwieldy craft were controlled by three long sweeps, one at the stern and one sticking out each side. It was from this arrangement that they were also called "broadhorns." It would draw about two feet of water when fully loaded. The flatboat had a deck, with living quarters in the stern complete with hearth and chimney. Their rugged construction made them bullet resistant, a welcome advan-

tage when attacked by marauding bands of Indians or the murderous white riff-raff that frequented the Ohio–Mississippi country. For offense, loopholes situated all around the hull allowed volleys of gunfire to be hailed on the attackers.

Around 1785 it was in such "boats" that men from Ohio, Kentucky and other regions of the western frontier carried cargoes of flour, pork, tobacco, hemp and iron down the Mississippi to the markets at Natchez and New Orleans, selling both their boats and cargo at their destination. Most of the early sidewalks of New Orleans were made from flatboat timber, as were some of the houses. Flatboats were also fitted out as mobile shops, smithys, toolmakers, barrooms and museums to serve the riverside communities. In the peak year of 1847, more than 2600 flatboats originating in the Ohio Valley were recorded as landing in the New Orleans area alone, hundreds more finding their way to other ports upriver.

In the early days the crews made their way back overland by the Natchez Trace, an overland trail. The Natchez Trace was a 450 mile trail between Natchez and Nashville, created by the crews returning upstream, and it was the only way home.

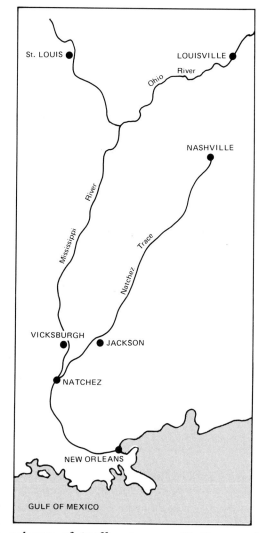

The Natchez Trace.

The volume of traffic grew until these colorful "Kaintuck" boatmen had trampled the trail into a crude road. From 1800 to 1820 this rough road was the most heavily travelled in the southwest. Boatmen, soldiers, postmen, missionaries, Indians and pioneer settlers moved along the road sharing its discomforts and dangers. Steaming swamps, floods, insects, accidents, sickness, unfriendly Indians and occasional robbers plagued the trace. It was to the robbers that many of the boatmen fell foul, returning home with the rewards of their trip, only to lose out on the way. Some, of course, paid with their lives. Today only a few sections of the original historic trace remain. It is now a tourist route and for the bulk of its run it is modern highway.

By 1819 there were as many as twenty steamboats operating between New Orleans and such
interior cities as St. Louis, Louisville, and Nashville, providing a safe and fast passage back up the
river, an alternative to the trace.

Flatboat on the Ohio River, ca. 1850.
(Courtesy Missouri Historical Society.)

"Cave in Rock" on the Ohio River.

Among the perils of the rivers was the "Cave in the Rock," located on the Ohio in the State of Illinois. It was a lair for pirates who preyed upon passing river traffic. This cave in a limestone bluff extended back one hundred and eight feet—it was in excess of forty feet wide and twenty-five feet high. The floor was very smooth throughout, and the walls rose in steps like seats in a theatre. Strange hieroglyphics dating back into prehistoric days covered the gloomy walls. The mystery of the cave was enhanced by another apartment over the cavern. Legend has it that around sixty human skeletons were found here. The passageway to this second cavern was like a huge chimney some fourteen feet long.

In the early days, the cave entrance was partially concealed by shrubs and bushes. It commanded a long view of the upper river, and it was simple to waylay New Orleans-bound flatboats. The boaters were easily lured in with offers of help and warnings of dangers ahead only to be expeditiously murdered and their cargoes pilfered by the pirates who finished the trip to New Orleans and collected the profits. Around 1810, so many crews and cargoes had disappeared that shippers in Pittsburgh sent

a force down river. This action helped considerably in cleaning out the robbers. The cave had also served as a home for early settlers and at a later date as an Inn, proclaimed by a sign, "Wilsons Liquor Vault and House of Entertainment."

Another pirate who plagued the Ohio was the infamous Colonel Plug. He tricked the unsuspecting flatboat crews by going upstream of his headquarters and pretending to be an unfortunate traveler marooned on the river bank. His impassioned appeals to be taken on board usually succeeded. Once aboard, he surreptitiously picked out the caulking from the seams of the boat, timing the operation so that the craft would sink near his headquarters. His henchman would then appear on the river bank and row out to save the Colonel and the cargo, leaving the crew to drown. The Colonel, however, got his just desserts when he miscalculated the timing and the boat sank before his henchmen arrived. That time, the Colonel followed his many victims to a watery grave.

A keelboat was built on conventional lines with sharp bow and stern. Constructed of heavy timbers and shallow of draught, it could carry from twenty to forty tons of freight. Unable to exploit the power of the winds and with the power of running water available only in a downstream direction, rivermen were handicapped by their reliance on human energy for upstream propulsion. This handicap was further accentuated by the great distances. Sails were of little value when navigating the shallow, winding, and often narrow rivers that formed the principal waterways. The advantage of swift currents for downstream traffic was largely nullified by the cost of labor moving boats back upstream. Upstream traffic had to be moved almost entirely by muscle power, and except for an occasional experiment with horse-drawn boats, the burden of this work fell upon man. It is hard to imagine a harder task than that of the keelboat crews who pushed, pulled, warped, cordelled and sometimes sailed their craft on their upstream journeys.

Warping was a process carried out by tying a long rope to a tree upstream, then hauling in the line to pull the boat up to the anchorage point. Cordelling was a method of moving a boat through banks of deep water lined with brush. A rope as much as one thousand feet long was made secure at the top of the mast. Such ropes were called cordelles. The boat was pulled along with this line by men on shore. In order to keep the boat from swinging around the mast, the line was connected to the bow of the boat by means of a "bridle," a short auxillary line fastened to a loop in the bow, and to a ring through which the cordelle was passed. The bridle prevented the boat from swinging under the force of the wind or current when the upstream speed of the boat was insufficient to accomplish this purpose by use of the rudder. It could take

Cordelling a keelboat.

from twenty to forty men to cordelle along average stretches of river.

Another method employed was that of "poling," using tough ash poles eighteen to twenty feet in length, with a wooden or iron shoe at one end to push against the bottom of the river, and on its upper end a crutch for the crewman's shoulder. Running along each side of the boat was a narrow cleated gangway. This was used as a walkway for a crew of four or five men who would thrust the poles into the river bottom and on command walk toward the stern while leaning on the poles, thereby propelling the boat forward in shallow water.

Whenever the opportunity presented itself a further method of making headway was that of "bushwacking," wherein the crew pulled themselves along by means of the bushes growing along the river bank. This method was also used to advantage when the river or stream was in flood, enabling the crew to navigate through the woods by grasping the branches of trees. Until the advent of the steamboat, keelboats were the only sizeable craft capable of hauling cargo upstream against the current.

Keelboat crews because of the nature of their jobs were a tough, rough, dissolute, unruly lot, and as one might expect, the period produced some legendary characters. One such character was Mike Fink. He was born near Pittsburgh around 1780, served as a scout in the Indian wars, and then worked up to the ownership of two keelboats. He was a most rugged individual, famous as the "King of the Keelboatmen." He was also known as the most boastful fighter, and the best rifleman among his compatriots. His river career lasted from around 1790 until his death. Some sources suggest that he was shot and killed as a young man, while others say that he lived until 1882. Among his many skills was that of being able to navigate his keelboat through the many rapids, a feat in which boatmen took particular pride. Mike Fink boasted, "I'm a salt river roarer! I'm a ringtailed squealer! I'm a reg'lar screamer from the ol' Massassip'! Whoop! I'm the very infant that refused his milk before its eyes were open, and called for a bottle of old Rye! I love the wimmin an' I'm chock ful' o' fight! I'm half wild horse and half cockeyed alligator and the rest o' me is crooked snags an' every lick I make in the woods lets in an acre o' sunshine. I can outrun, outjump, outshoot, outbrag, outdrink an' outfight, rough-an-tumble, no holds barred, any man on both sides the river from Pittsburgh to New Orleans an' back again to St. Louiee. Come on you flatters, you bargers, you milk-white mechanics an' see how tough I am to chaw! I ain't had a fight for two days an' I' spilein' for exercise! Cock-a-doodle-doo!"

If there was one sort of fighting on the Ohio River more typical of the flatboat era than any other it was an encounter between whites on board a boat and Indians along the shore near which the boat had drifted or been brought by means of a decoy. It was rare that Indians ventured on the river to attack a boat on even terms. All their skilled cunning centered in luring the crews ashore. Perhaps the most successful ruse employed to make boats come to shore was by compelling renegades or white captives to act as decoys; these unfortunate and sometimes treacherous persons would appear at the water's edge and implore to be saved by passing boats. The decoys would hail the boat from the riverbank begging to be taken aboard. To add substance to their act, they would relate where and when they had been taken captive and how they made their escape, adding that the Indians were hot on their trail. Should the crew fall for his trick and pull into shore, the Indians would break cover, fire a fusillade of gunshots, board the boat, massacre the crew, and plunder the cargo.

Mimicking the call of the turkey was a common decoy used by Indians. From an early age they were trained to become proficient in this art. The thought of a tasty meal roused by the gobbling of 'turkeys' in the woods lured the boat and crew ashore to find only too late that they had fallen into a deadly trap.

Despite the rapid progress of the paddle steamer, its large cargo capacity and, by the standards of the day, its efficiency, it did not quickly displace the older river craft. Flatboats, keelboats and rafts not only survived but increased in numbers and importance in some fields. As flatboats were only used in downstream trades they were slower to feel the effects of steamboat competition. Flatboats however, had a substantial draught of water when loaded, it restricted their use on many streams to brief periods in the spring and autumn when they could be sent off on flood waters. The keelboats lingered on for decades. Their shallow draught allowed them to be operated on streams too shallow for steamboats and at seasons when the paddle steamers, even on the larger rivers found it difficult if not impossible to run. They served many isolated communities on the upper waters of the tributary streams bringing up manufactured goods and groceries, returning with produce to markets further down river. As late as 1840 keelboats were still arriving at Pittsburgh at the rate of eight a day. On rivers beset by rapids, empty keelboats were towed and as the need arose to reduce the draught of the paddle steamer to enable it to clear the obstacle, cargo was off-loaded into them and subsequently re-loaded. The paddle steamer was the first truly commercial boat to operate, and it greatly influenced the country's development in and around the rivers. It opened up a vast part of the land previously inaccessible other than by a long overland trek through territory beset by dangers from Indians, outlaws and the extremes of the climate. It was instrumental as the principal technological agent, in the development of the greater part of the vast Mississippi basin from a raw frontier society to economic and social maturity.

The *Western Engineer*. This was the first steamboat to ascend the Missouri, and was designed to strike terror in the hearts of Indians. Her best speed was three miles per hour, but Missouri River mud clogged her boiler, necessitating frequent stops. It is not known whether or not she impressed the Indians or deterred them.

The paddle steamer like many mechanical inventions was the product of many men. It would be wrong to try to single out any one personality, but two names repeatedly appear when the pages of paddle steamer history are turned. Robert Fulton and John Fitch. Robert Fulton has been generally credited with the invention of the steamboat. He in turn owed a great deal to James Watt, who developed the steam engine; without such a prime mover, there could have been no steamboat. Fulton's *Clermont* launched in 1807 was 130 feet long, with a 16 foot beam and a hull depth of 7 feet. The engine had a cylinder 24 inches in diameter with a 4 foot stroke. It powered paddle wheels 15 inches in diameter with a two foot dip. It should be noted that dimensions and descriptions of this craft vary. A drawing by John Wolcott Adams showed the *Clermont* as a side-wheeler. At a later stage, her beam was increased to 18 feet and she was renamed *North River*.

Robert Fulton's *Clermont*, 1807. The first truly successful steamboat. The following announcement was made in the *American Citizen*, New York, August 17, 1807: "Mr. Fulton's ingenious steamboat, invented with a view to navigation of the Mississippi from New Orleans upward, sails today from the North River, near States Prison, to Albany. The velocity is calculated at four miles an hour. It is said that it will make progress of two against the current of the Mississippi and if so it will certainly be a very valuable acquisition to the commerce of Western States." She made the trip from New York City to Albany in 32 hours.

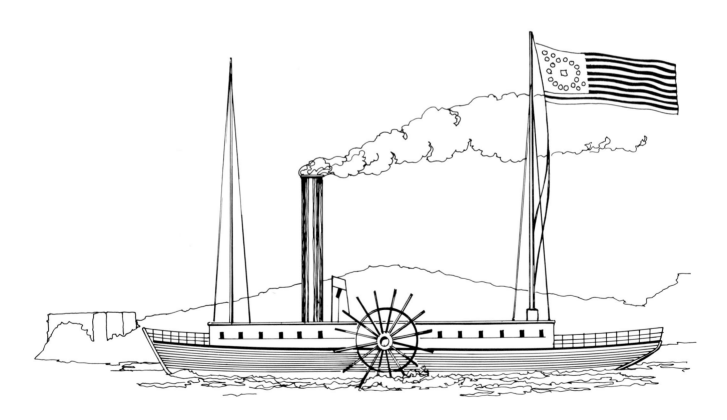

John Fitch, an inventor born at Windsor, Connecticut, settled down after years of roaming, on the banks of the Delaware River, where in 1785 he conceived a steamboat. The first boat designed by Fitch was 45 feet in length, with vertical paddles working at the sides; his second ship, built in 1788, was 60 feet long and had similar paddles, only this time placed at the stern. In 1792 another inventor, Elijah Ormsbee, a Connecticut Yankee residing at Rhode Island and financed by a man named David Wilkinson, built a small steamboat at Windsors Cove, Narragansett Bay, employing an "atmospheric engine" and "duck's foot" paddles. It attained a speed of three miles an hour. The invention of the atmospheric engine is usually attributed to Thomas Newcomen, a blacksmith of Dartford, England.

Rober Fulton and his partner Robert Livingstone held a patent, granted by the state of New York, in 1810 giving them sole rights to navigate the rivers of that state by steamship. They obtained similar rights from the state of Louisiana for the New Orleans area. One of Fulton's ambitions was to obtain a complete monopoly of river navigation in return for providing what was then to be a fast and reliable steamboat service between New Orleans and Pittsburgh. He did in fact make many such agreements with other states. The first to challenge this monopoly was Captain Shreve with his boat *George Washington*. After a very long legal battle he won his case, the start of many such challenges by other interested parties. Enterprising steamboat builders and operators successfully foiled his plans until the cost in time and money caused him to withdraw from the controversy.

With the advent of the paddle wheel steamboat, a great expanse of fertile land opened up. Access to that land was very difficult, but the problems were overcome by the drive, initiative, and adventurous spirit of a new pioneer, the riverman. The steamboat era really opened up when a Captain H.M. Shreve piloted the first mechanically successful steamboat down the Ohio River in September 1816. Named the *Washington*, she measured 150 feet long, with a 24 foot beam and a hull depth of 6 feet. This shallow draught was made possible by placing the engines on the deck and flooring over the hull. She was a side-wheeler, and the main cabin was 60 feet long, containing some forty double berths.

With the increase in the numbers of steamboats, the inevitable happened; being faster, the steamboats absorbed the entire river commerce, and most of the individual boatmen went out of business. Some found work as deck hands or pilots on the new steamers. Others crewed the large coal flats or pine rafts that floated down the rivers. Mark Twain, in his book *Life on the Mississippi* describes the passage of just such craft that floated down the river, past his home town of Hannibal, remarking on the wigwam type tents erected on the rafts as shelter form the elements.

Highways did not penetrate into the midwest until many years later, and the Mississippi Valley depended upon the large and small steamboats long after the railroads had come to share transportation in other regions. Steamboats could not only get pioneers and their chattels into previously inaccessible areas, they could also provide fast transport of the pioneers' products back to the markets.

The shallow hulls of the steamers did not require wharfs or ports to load and unload cargo, so all the traditional essentials for landings were discarded. The paddle steamer could move cargo virtually anywhere along the bank. In time villages formed at the popular landing points, then developed into towns. When the rivers were obstructed by rapids and the like, other communities sprang up at the alternative landing points to fulfill the needs of tranship cargoes. Boatbuilding communities were also born at the advent of the steamboat, and the whole country surged forward on a new wave of progress.

Horse powered paddle steamers, sometimes referred to as "hay burners" were operated as ferries in the 1880s. They were small in size with side wheels powered by a horse turning a treadmill. Detailed information on these unique craft has proved difficult to obtain, but the Howard Yard of Jeffersonville, Indiana reported building one in 1800. One attempt was made to start an up-river service with horse driven boats from New Orleans to Louisville. The project was abandoned at an early stage, too many horses were used up.

Mississippi River steamboats competed successfully with railroads for the passenger and freight

A tank barge tow moving up the Ohio River near
Wheeling, West Virginia. The barges are being
pushed by the towboat *Goldfinch* owned by Dravo
Mechling Corporation, Pittsburgh, Pennsylvania.
(Courtesy, The American Waterways Operators, Inc.)

business for many years after the first railroad tracks were laid into the territory. Eventually, however, the steamboat in its turn was made obsolete by the advance of the railroad. In the years 1830 to 1840, track miles jumped from 23 to 2,808. The following decade added a further 3,400 miles, and by the mid-fifties they totalled over 9,000 miles. Tracks were laid to suit traffic requirements. No longer was progress tied to the river. The railroad was a more reliable and faster means of travel, and it eroded the steamboat trade until by the late eighties, the steamboats had faded into the past.

The railroads, however, were to suffer a similar fate as a result of automobile and air transport, both of which took lucrative business from the railroad.

Towboats put bulk cargo back on the rivers when locks and dams were constructed which permitted the movement of large barge tows over great distances. The railroad could not compete with the low costs of this operation.

The modern river barge measures 195 feet long by 35 feet wide and 12 feet deep. The present locks can accommodate a tow vessel and fifteen such

The main lock at McAlpine Locks, located on the Ohio River near Louisville, Kentucky. The lock is 110 feet wide, 1200 feet long and lifts or lowers to compensate for the thirty-seven foot difference in levels between the upper and lower rivers.

barges with ease, as they measure 1,200 feet by 110 feet. A tow-barge combination of this size would be a quarter of a mile long. By comparison it would require a train of two and three-quarter miles in length, and by road, nine hundred trucks—which with a spacing of a hundred and fifty feet, would stretch thirty six miles.

The diesel-powered towboat has been responsible for bringing the use of rivers back into prominence, the paddle wheel having been replaced by propellers. Placed above the water level in a recess in the hull, propellers draw water up and thrust the boat forward. The performance has been further improved by the addition of the "kort nozzle," a device that concentrates the flow of water through the prop blade, thereby adding considerable thrust to the propeller drive.

Federal Barge Lines, who specialize in this type of traffic, has among its fleet two boats, the *America* and the *United States*, each craft having nine thousand horse power from four engines, and the capabilities of pushing nearly fifty thousand tons. (It should be noted that the term towboat usually refers to a boat pushing its tow. A tow of this size would cover six acres, and move at speeds of up to fifteen miles per hour.

2

THE PADDLE STEAMER

The steam-powered river boat was the first American invention of world significance; the first technical accomplishment that freed man from the limitations placed upon his movements up and down rivers by the vagaries of the wind. It accelerated the advance of the commercial frontier to some 2,000 miles west, from the Appalachians to the Rockies.

The first paddle wheel was very likely simply an axle with paddles radiating outward, adequately braced to exert thrust when the axle was rotated by any suitable means. It was an improvement upon the six perpendicular paddles on either side of the boat, that John Fitch first hitched to steam power in July 1736. The mechanism of Fitch's Philadelphia Boat was described as follows: "The cylinder is horizontal, the steam working with equal force at both ends. The piston moves about three feet and each vibration gives the axis forty revolutions. Each revolution of the axis moves twelve oars or paddles five and a half feet; they work perpendicularly and are represented by the strokes of the paddle of a canoe. As six paddles are raised from the water six more are entered, and the two sets of paddles make their strokes of about eleven feet in each direction. The crank of the axis acts upon the paddles about one third of their length from the lower ends to which part of the oar the whole force of the axis is applied. The engine is placed in the bottom of the boat, about one third from the stern, and both the action and the reaction turn the wheel the same way."

The paddle wheel innovation may perhaps be credited to one Samuel Mory of Connecticut, who certainly used one on the eight steamboats to be built in America in the year 1797. The river steamboat was not just one type of craft, but a multitude of designs covering short haul passenger and freight, floating palaces, ferries, train ferries, snagboats, dredgers and towboats. Most dominant were the packet boats, combination passenger and freight haulers, which ranged from insignificant tubs making trips of only ten miles to huge floating palaces operating between ports a thousand miles apart. Some, fitted with a wooden sloping superstructure, and metal clad, became the gunboats of

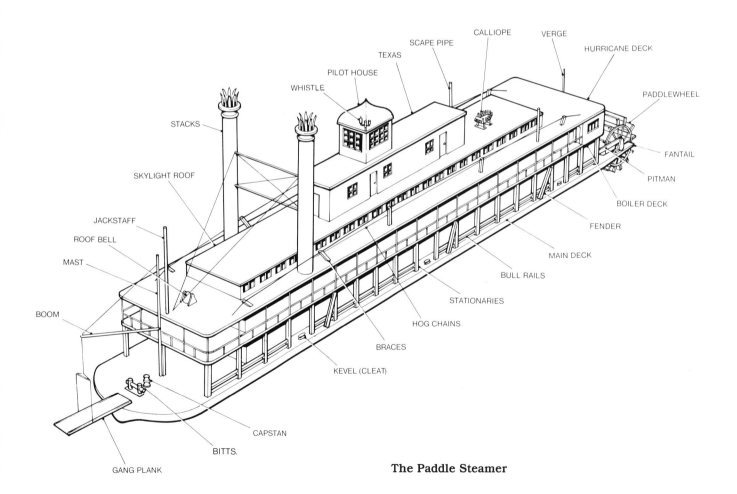

The Paddle Steamer

John Fitch's experimental steamboat
using vertical paddles.

the Civil War. Even the original design was often changed at the whim of the owner, possibly to meet some unforeseen requirement with the result that rarely can one find two identical photographs of the same boat. However, the originals did follow a basic pattern. Long narrow hulls, for instance, were found to be faster as well as easier to handle in shallow water and in the swift current of the rapids. The timber hulls, however, had a common structural problem—the arching of the hull known as "hogging." This was caused by a distortion from the weight of the machinery and cargo, or from the shocks when grounding or snagging occurred. The solution was a combination of hog chains, trusses and bulkheads, or a series of small, arched hog frames tied by rods. Hog chains were iron rods made fast to the hull timbers at bow and stern and carried over a series of struts rising from the keelsons. These could be adjusted for rigidity by means of turnbuckles to tighten the hull and to prevent arching or sagging. Cross chains were used in a similar manner to support the wide guards usually found on side-wheelers overhanging the hull. Yet the casual observer would have to look hard to see evidence of this internal structure among all the decorations that adorned the steamboat. Out of this confusion of designs two basic types, the side-wheeler and stern-wheeler evolved. The reasons for,

and the mechanics of these different types are dealt with in a subsequent chapter. Basically the external appearance was that of a series of boxes in aesthetic white dropped on to a black barge. The lower deck was fitted out with practical guards and bullrails, whilst the upper deck boasted a profusion of decorative woodwork referred to as "gingerbread," "jigsaw," or "pseudo gothic." In appearance the steamboat frequently justified a humorist's definition of it as "an engine on a raft with 11,000 dollars worth of jig-saw work." These highly embellished designs and accommodations reached their zenith after the Civil War in boats such as the *Grand Republic* and the *J. M. White III*, (some of the larger boats of the period even had libraries). The whole assembly was topped off with two gigantic chimney stacks. The first deck, (main deck) accommodated the boilers and machinery, and provided space for the varied cargo that these boats were wont to carry. The next deck, the boiler deck, supported the main cabin and staterooms. Above this was the hurricane deck through which the main cabin skylight projected, the roof of which, naturally was called the skylight roof. Atop the skylight roof was the "texas," a series of cabins providing accommodation for the crew, the captain's cabin being situated at the forward end. The skylight roof and that of the texas was covered with

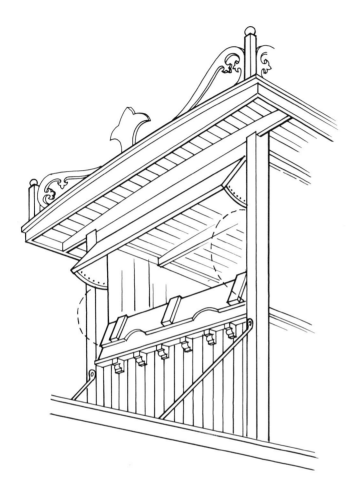

The pilot house. Until the perfection of good window glass in the 1920s pilot house fronts were open, summer and winter. A system of wooden boards was used to close this opening. The uppermost was the browboard or visor. It was hinged at the top of swing outward to keep the sun out of the pilot's eyes. It was held open by pins in the wood quadrants at the sides. Below the visor was the breastboard, which was hinged at the bottom and met the lower edge of the visor when both were closed. The half moons cut out on the top edge of the breastboard enabled the pilot to peek through when the pilot house was buttoned up.

canvas treated with a mixture of paint and sand, making it fire resistant to the many sparks falling from the chimneys. The texas roof supported an elaborately windowed cabin called the pilot house. Its main component was the large wheel, up to twelve feet in diameter to turn the rudders and steer the boat. This was the pilot's domain where he would spend many lonely hours at the wheel. He signalled his instructions to the engine room by means of bell pulls. The boat's whistle was usually operated by a floor-mounted pedal in the pilot house. A bell of some size was located on the hurricane deck mounted forward of the chimneys. It was originally used for communication between steamboats, but the clarity and audibility varied with atmospheric conditions. Frequently misunderstood or not heard, the bell often contributed to confusion that resulted in collisions. The introduction of the steam whistle brought about a marked reduction of accidents. Every boat had a whistle toned and tuned to be distinguished from other boats of the same line. The whistles were melodious and wide-ranged instruments. Some blew chords, others a succession of notes, still others a combination of both. Riverside folk could identify the boats by the sound of their whistles: some also claimed that they could identify the pilot by the way he operated the whistle.

Other fixtures in this navigation center included a wood-burning potbellied stove, a "lazy bench" across the back, and sometimes a spittoon and a water cooler. The lazy bench usually accommodated visiting pilots, some just there for the ride, others improving their knowledge of the river and its latest pitfalls. It was also the center from which some of the tallest stories originated for talk was free and it filled the long watches.

Although many pilot houses were flat-topped with little ornamentation except for trim at the corners, some of the finer boats had open domes formed by lacy arches and could be mistaken for fancy summer houses. The peaks of these sometimes supported elaborate finials which often took the form of eagles, statues or gold balls. On the *Belle of Alton* the dome was surmounted by a large crescent moon.

The bell of the *City of Cincinnati*, typical of the type used to signal departures, fog warnings, fire and boat drill alarms. Usually positioned forward on the upper deck.

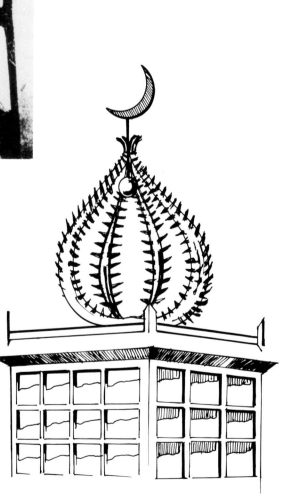

The Pilot house decoration on the *Belle of Alton*.

The side-wheeler *Grand Republic* near St. Louis, 1876, built in 1867 at Pittsburgh and called the *Great Republic*. In 1872 her hull and beam were extended and she was outfitted as the most luxuriously appointed boat on the river. She was completely destroyed by fire in 1877. Of particular interest were the stained glass windows in the cupola atop her pilot house. (Courtesy of the collection of the Public Library of Cincinnati and Hamilton County.)

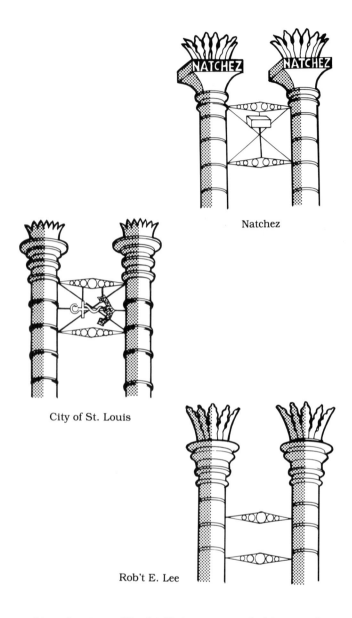

Natchez

City of St. Louis

Rob't E. Lee

The ultimate in this art form was possibly a tall cupola with stained glass windows on top of the *Grand Republic's* pilot house. The chimney stacks themselves usually had decorative tops. Ornamental oak leaves, feathers, rings and pointed crowns were popular chimney top decorations, sometimes called bonnets or petticoat tops. The high chimneys, a common feature of the paddle steamer were designed to give boilers increased draught. The standard maximum height of the chimneys in 1840 was fifty feet above the river surface. On larger boats, such as the *Grand Republic* launched in 1867, the height was increased to one hundred feet. The framed formed by the spreaders between the stacks, was an ideal and prominent place in which to mount the company insignia. Anchor line boats had an anchor silhouette, while large gold balls were the mark of the Eagle Packet Company's fleet.

To enter the larger riverboats such as the Grand Republic, was to take a step into another world. The long narrow saloon typically included a ceiling with a mass of curved filigree woodwork touched up with elaborate gilding. From it were suspended big chandeliers with their multitude of pendants glittering like rainbows, and the light from the colored glazing of the skylights bounced off the pendants and around the fairy tale vista. It was truly a magnificent sight, further enhanced by a double row of columns on each side, which supported more elaborately gilded arches. The long saloon invariably had a large mirror at one end adding a further dimension of depth. Each side would be flanked by staterooms, each door sporting an individual oil painting set above a porcelain knob, the whole set in an elaborate portico. It is generally believed that the term "stateroom" originated on the steamboats, when the numbered cabins were named after the states of the Union. The saloon was also the dining room and lounge around which the social life of the boat revolved. The rear of this resplendent tunnel accommodated the ladies' cabin, tastefully decorated and fitted with a deep pile carpet. Large mirrors would be fitted around the walls. The gentlemen's saloon occupied the forward end, with a bar off to the side. The bars were usually leased from the boats owners. It was a saying on the river that if a man owned a bar on a popular packet, it was better than possessing a gold mine. In fact,

Steamboatmen liked tall, fancy-topped chimneys because of their impressive appearance, but they contended that tall stacks were necessary to toss sparks high and to give a good draught to the furnaces. Ornamental oak leaves and pointed crowns were popular chimney top decorations (sometimes called bonnets or petticoat tops). The iron bars between the chimneys served as braces or spreaders. The space between the spreaders was an ideal place on which to mount the company's insignia, which took many forms: balls, horse shoes, anchors, stars, cotton bales, or circles.

Pilot house. It was said that every time a riverman told the truth, one of his ears would fall off; earless rivermen were seldom, if ever, seen.

men who owned life leases of steamboat bars willed them to their sons as their richest legacies. These elegant bars were the settings for the legendary professional gambler, dressed in fancy clothes taking the innocents for a ride. The stories surrounding these men, however, were more fiction than fact, but when they were caught cheating, the offending gamblers were put ashore at the earliest opportunity. At least one such gambler was known to have jumped overboard to flee the wrath of his accusers. Gambling disputes, illicit sexual relations, and theft presented a problem to the paddle steamer crews who dealt with the violations severely. Occasionally more serious offences had to be reckoned with, especially on the lower deck where conditions were wretched. Here the mix of emi-

grant families, flatboatmen and deckhands frequently led to quarrels and fighting. Manslaughter, murder, and rape were occasionally committed, but the more common offences were swindling and theft. In cases of murder, where the culprit was known, he would be apprehended and handed over to the law at the next town. The customary penalties for other offences were flogging and putting ashore. Often the passengers themselves meted out additional punishment. This rough and ready justice reflected the age of the frontiersman.

There were many tales of thievery on boats. One in particular concerned the steamer, *John Raine*. The boat was en route from New Orleans to Louisville in 1857, when a series of thefts occurred among the deck passengers. The enraged victims, some thirty in number formed a committee which then ordered a search of all the persons on deck. One man, a stranger, declined the invitation and jumped overboard. He was subsequently recaptured and convicted after most of the stolen money was found on him. He was sentenced to run the gauntlet, had his head shaved, and was stripped of all his clothing except his pants. He was then viciously whipped and chased from the stern to the bow of the boat at which point the unfortunate and desperate miscreant again jumped overboard. He was spotted later on the riverbank.

Because of the general public's reticence in reporting such matters, the extent of illicit sexual relations was difficult to determine but does not appear to have been a major problem. The practice of prostitution was either negligible, very well concealed, or ignored. Such occurrences when discovered were summarily dealt with by the boats' officers, and/or, outraged passengers.

The main saloon could consume as much as a third of the total operating expenses but this was not always so. Accommodation in the early days consisted of curtained berths down each side of the main cabin, with a similar layout at the rear for the ladies. The next move was the provision of a few special cabins with individual accommodation. Each cabin would be a room about six foot square housing two bunks. Crude ablutions were provided in an adjacent room with tin basins, roller towels and the use of not-too-clean river water. This in turn was superceded by hot and cold running water and steam heating. Potbellied stoves, even in the latter years were, in the main, the only form of heating, and were usually located in the main saloon and adjoining social rooms. Others were located in the texas and pilot house. The cabins eventually became larger, were equipped with more conventional furniture and decorated to the point of being gaudy. In the early days, most cabins sported a list of regulations the content of which was usually aimed at men. "Gentlemen" were forbidden to lie down in berths with boots on, to appear coatless at the table, to enter the ladies' cabin without the ladies' consent, to whittle or otherwise damage the furniture and so on. Gambling however, was permitted on most boats; some displayed signs such as "Gentlemen who play cards for money, do so at their own risk." Some boats carried signs

"Games for money strictly forbidden" and then turned a blind eye unless fellow passengers complained.

At peak times, to house the overflow, even the main saloon would be carpeted with passengers sleeping on mattresses spread over the floor. The main saloon, when set out as a dining room, could compete with any first class hotel of the day, with exquisite china, shining silver and sparkling cut glass laid out on dazzling white tablecloths. The food served up on the steamboats varied from slop to that of the best French restaurants. This depended upon kitchen facilities and the owner's selection of, or the availability of, good kitchen staff. A doubtful source of labor was available among the many European immigrants flooding into America at this time. Sometimes hunters were engaged as members of the crew to rustle game for the menu. They performed no other duties. Typical meals for full fare paying passengers on the better class of boats were quite wide in their selection, although very often badly balanced. Breakfast offered a choice of beef steaks, fowl, pigeon, ragout, plates of sliced meats including ham, and coffee or tea. For dinner, baked pork or turkey, huge platters of beef steaks, small platters of duck, chicken or other fowl, plates of cold sliced meat, potatoes, rice and corn, a selection of tarts and rice pudding, coffee and tea. Supper was usually along the same lines as breakfast. Milk as well as butter was often lacking, or poor in quality. The most frequent complaint was that steamboat meals were very coarsely prepared, and often greasy.

When stirred up and mixed the Mississippi River, water was considered an invigorating potion (this of course in the days before towns began discharging sewage into the river). Passengers aware of the water's reputation would embark with kegs, jigs or demijohns filled from wells or cisterns. Some boats carried a "settling barrell" at the stern, where river water dipped up in buckets was allowed to settle before drinking. River silt along with other odds and ends including small fish would accumulate in the bottom.

Music on the steamboats ranged from the hoarse whistles of the calliope, to a stringed orchestra in the cabin. Some boats tried brass bands; however, while these attracted some customers they were expensive, and therefore eventually dropped as unprofitable. The cabin orchestra was the cheaper and most enduring, plus the best drawing card. A band of six or eight black men who could play the violin, banjo or guitar and sing well was always a good investment. These men were paid to work as waiters, barbers and baggagemen, but were granted the privilege of passing round the hat occasionally and splitting their reward. They made good wages by this combination. A good orchestra would add to the patronage.

Utilities slowly progressed to better quality. Illumination started with candles, moved to whale oil lamps then to gas lamps supplied from gas manufactured aboard. Some very elaborate crystal chandeliers supporting countless pendants, had oil lamps as their source. Finally the electric light made its appearance. Washing facilities in the early days were poor. Tin wash basins and roller towels, located in the barber shop were all that was available. Toilets were usually of the outhouse variety, located toward the stern of the boat. They were eventually replaced by more modern plumbing equipment.

The world of the full fare paying passengers contrasted vividly with that of the lower deck passengers, traveling at a much cheaper rate. The latter were accommodated, if that was the word, in competition with the deck crew, in a few rough bunks, or they hunted out nooks and crannies among the cargo. They shared a communal stove on which to cook their food. In some cases deck passengers could obtain a further reduction in fares by working their passage. In reality this put them at the beck and call of the deck crew at any hour, in any weather fair or foul. Often they had to take on the cords of wood to fuel the hungry boilers, or transship cargo over very muddy banks. Frequent overcrowding caused conditions which gave rise to comments such as, "the black hole" or "treated like hogs." Needless to say the filth and stench were breeding grounds for numerous diseases including cholera, which found an ideal carrier in the deck where poor conditions encouraged epidemics. The fear of catching cholera was often the reason for wholesale desertion by crews. And during these outbreaks of disease, slave owners, fearing loss to their assets quickly withdrew slaves hired out as steamboat hands.

To a lesser degree, yellow fever also made an appearance, but since it was prevalent when the weather was hot, a time when, due to low water, the steamboat traffic was light, it did not prove such a menace. Smallpox too showed itself occasionally, and it was not until after the Civil War that some towns on the Mississippi established quarantine regulations to counteract the problem.

Deck passengers suffered a high casualty rate from accidents. Their position put them amidst burst steam pipes, exploding boilers, and collapsing flue pipes. They were right in line to be catapulted out of the boat or be hit by flying parts of a fractured cylinder head. Their deck, piled high with cargo with every corner filled, would be the first to submerge should there be a collision. In later years regulations were introduced which resulted in improvements, thus bettering the lot of crews and passengers alike, for even in those early days the deck crews frequently went on strike to improve their conditions. One such significant improvement was the introduction of wide gang planks, swung out on booms. Prior to this, access to and from the boats for passengers and cargo was by loose planks, often very slippery, supported by trestles or boxes—a very doubtful arrangement when crossing deep mud, the usual condition away from paved levees.

One of the main cargoes of the steamboat was bales of cotton. Some of the larger boats carried as many as 9,000 bales a trip. With this sort of load aboard, little could be seen of the boat itself. The bales, stacked just above the water line, rose up and sometimes above the top deck. A passenger on a successful cotton boat could make the entire trip in his cabin without seeing the light of day.

In the port, the volume of traffic called for better loading facilities. Some took the form of wharf boats, or old steamboat hulls. Others paved levees up to a mile in length, extending from the top of the bank right down to below the water's edge. The traffic to be accommodated, was measured at St. Louis in 1845 as 1,872 boats arriving. This increased to 3,184 by 1852.

Steamboats in the early days relied a great deal for their trade on casual pickups along the river banks. The recognized signal during the day was waving of a white handkerchief or a loud "hello there." During the dark hours, a lantern, a blazing torch, or log was used. Riverboat crews also deliv-

Cotton was king on the south-western waters. Boats were loaded to the pilot house with cotton, and behind the bales, passengers traveled by lamplight. This cotton packet, the *America*, was built in 1898 for Captain Le Verrier Cooley, who ran her in trades out of New Orleans. She was used in the film "Magnolia" in 1924. She foundered at New Orleans, August, 1924. (Courtesy of Southern Comfort Corporation.)

A torch basket.

ered small parcels and letters to isolated riverside dwellers, and it was not unknown for the boats to receive shouted instructions from the shore to "bring me up a barrel of flour or a keg of sugar," to be dropped off on the return journey. Prior to the 1870s steamboats used torch baskets for lighting the nearby shores, both on the rare occasions for night navigation (because of the treacherous river conditions most boats were moored up at night) and night landings. The torch, a wrought iron lattice basket, about a foot in diameter, and eighteen inches deep, swung loosely between the prongs of a forked iron bar or standard, which could be set in sockets in the foredeck, leaning far out over the water so as to allow live embers from the burning wood to fall into the river and not upon the deck.

They were fuelled with pine knots, split "light" wood," or "fat wood." The resinous sap in the wood burned fiercely, making a bright light. The addition of a ladle with pulverized resin would create an even fiercer flame, momentarily increasing the brilliance. A night landing was a picturesque and animated scene—the loading of the wide variety of cargo, the shouted orders to the roustabouts, the hiss of escaping steam, and all the sights and sounds of the passengers embarking and disembarking. With the boats departure, only the silent levee with the ripples of the water breaking on the beach would disturb the quiet, as the faint glimmer of the watchman's lantern illuminated the darkness.

Thealka, built at Paintsville, Kentucky, on the Big Sandy in 1899, and named after Alka Meek, daughter of the owner Captain Meek. The sign painter erroneously ran The Alka together creating her unusual name. *Thealka* was known as "bat wing one-stacker." Note the lanterns mounted on the roof. (From the collection of the Public Library of Cincinnati and Hamilton County.)

Around 1850 the coal oil or whale oil lantern came into use. This was just like a locomotive headlight with a case large enough for a children's playhouse. At first these lanterns were mounted at each corner of the roof aimed at the shore. Eventually they were mounted on a turntable which the pilot turned with a sashcord. With the advent of electrical power, searchlights were installed and provided a great advantage for night navigation and safety. When operating at night and in conditions of poor visibility, the pilot would sometimes order the stokehold to be screened as the reflected glare could throw confusing shadows.

With the progress of the steamboat the river became the main highway, and anything from chickens to a dismantled roundabout could be waiting on the bank for shipment. Very often the load had to be carried over, or through deep mud. It was from this situation that the apprentice clerk logging the goods aboard became known as "mud clerk." During its pre-Civil War heyday, it was said that the American river fleet carried more tonnage annually than that carried by all ships of the British Empire in the days when Britannia ruled the waves. It would be an almost impossible task to arrive at the number of paddle steamers operating at any one time on the western rivers. A good guide would be the numbers built: from the year 1811 to 1920 the total of all craft built on these rivers was around 12,000. It is assumed that the majority of the boats built were paddle steamers. The peak year of 1871 saw one hundred and fifty-five launchings. Because the screw propeller was ill-adapted for shallow waters, paddle wheels were the obvious choice, and due to their rugged construction they could usually survive punishment from obstructions. The nature of their construction enabled repairs, when needed, to be carried out by the crew from such materials and tools as were readily available. Side-wheelers had a more solid foundation than stern-wheelers since the paddles were placed midship, reducing hull stresses and counteracting excessive buoyancy. A major factor was that of maneuverability, i.e., problems with handling and turning. A side wheel boat when maneuvering at landings, locks or negotiating very sharp bends operated with one paddle wheel backing, and the other going ahead. A stern-wheeler was often compelled to "flank" around the elbow by backing against the point and letting the current swing the bow around the bend.

The earliest stern-wheelers were built by Daniel French and Henry Shreve, probably to get around the patents held by Robert Fulton, the inventor of the original paddleboats. Stern-wheelers fell from favor in the 1830s, staging a comeback in the early 1840s. On the whole these stern-wheelers were small craft, mainly used on the narrow tributaries. However, once the problem of supporting the heavy stern-wheelers aft was solved, they came into general use on larger boats. An advantage to using stern-wheelers was that of their pushing power, making them a superior towboat and enabling large cargoes to be moved on dumb barges, or unpowered hulls. Rear positioned paddles had the hull to protect them from floating debris, and the hull and side wheel guards could be widened and reduced to a more suitable size.

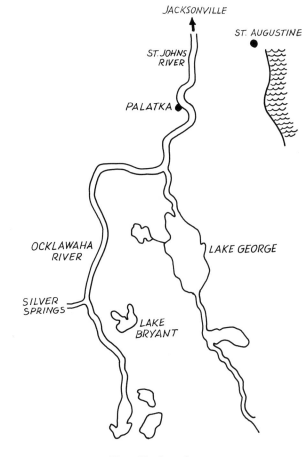

The *Okahumkee*

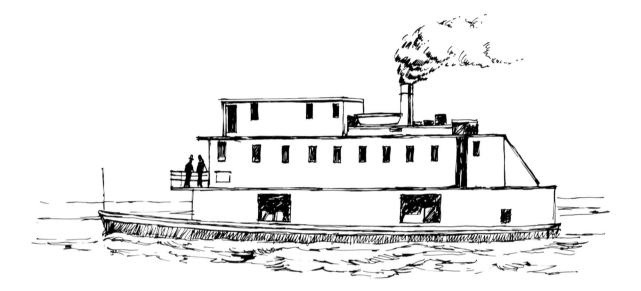

The *Okahumkee* is not a Mississippi River steam-boat but is included for two justifiably outstanding reasons. *Okahumkee* was possibly the longest lived wooden-hulled stern-wheeler of any period anywhere and she was propelled by a fully recessed stern wheel.

Built at Palatka, Florida in 1873 she last ran in 1920 having survived forty-seven years of operations. *Okahumkee* took her name from a legendary Indian chief, ruler of the tribes "around the south western lakes." The first boat of the "Hart Line," she suffered much rebuilding and remodelling during her life time. Some sources quote her length as eighty-four feet with a beam of twenty-one feet. She generated steam in a locomotive type boiler seventeen feet eight inches long by four feet diameter having a working pressure of one hundred fifteen pounds.

Her principle field of operations centered on the Ocklawaha River which ran through dark and gloomy forests, typical of the cypress swamps common to the area. She carried both freight and passengers, the latter accommodated in a few small but comfortable cabins. The sides of the Ocklawaha River boats were invariably rubbed glassy smooth or torn and creased by the friction of the bushes and trees that lined the banks of the river, and through which the boats had to forge a path. The paddle wheels of this type of boat were so recessed as to be completely invisible from abeam. It is assumed that this design was adopted to eliminate the possibility of the projecting bushes and trees from fouling the paddle wheel. Recessed paddle wheels were extreme rarities away from the Ocklawaha, on that stream they were a matter of course.

Success of steamboat builders, in reducing draught in relation to tonnage and cargo, resulted in a steady lengthening of the navigable season for steamboats of a given class. The expertise developed by steamboatmen in handling their craft during periods of low water further extended the seasons of steamboat operation. The stern wheel did create a steering problem, but this was overcome to some degree by the balanced rudder, i.e., as much surface forward as rear of the rudder axis. It did nevertheless, steer better in reverse, but the experienced pilot handled the boats without difficulty. From the mid-1800s when steamboats abounded on the rivers, up to the present, it is believed that the fleet has been reduced to only five in operation. They are the *Belle of Louisville* out of Louisville, Kentucky; the *Julia Bell Swain* out of Peoria, Illinois; the *Natchez* out of New Orleans; the *Mississippi Queen* and the *Delta Queen* out of New Orleans and Cincinatti respectively. Many of the old boats are now permanently moored up and down the rivers, serving as theatres and museums. Many other small ones have been converted into houseboats, but new small diesel-powered, day-excursion stern-wheelers are, to the delight of the tourists, threshing their way over the routes of the old timers, the river never losing its charm. The passengers would no doubt find it hard to envision the sheer numbers of boats that the old river scenes portrayed. The size and capacity of steamboats increased during the mid-1800s and culminated in the 365 foot *Eclipse* of 1853. The largest steamboat on the Mississippi which was designed but never built, was a 450 foot side-wheeler designed by the one Charles Ward during the fabulous twenties.

3

PADDLE STEAMER INTERIORS

The interior decoration and fittings of paddle steamers ranged from the bare basic essentials on the smaller craft to the extravagant opulence of the floating palaces. Elaborate as the exterior was apt to be, the architectural gem of the steamboat was its main cabin or grand saloon. During the 1840s and 50s the steamboat saloon grew from forty feet to about two hundred in length, and in the process became increasingly ornate in the owners effort to dazzle and astonish the public. The saloon extended through the center of the boiler deck and along almost its entire length, as befitting its function as the centerpiece of the steamboat. It served as a combination dining room and drawing room decorated in the most ornamental manner. The saloon had an air of spaciousness because of its height and vaulting although it was not usually very wide. The ceiling, elaborately decorated with frescoes, rosettes, diamonds, half diamonds and pendant acorns all painted in rich colors, was supported by rows of ornate columns with their connecting carved arches. On each side of the main saloon were rows of stateroom doors opening into individual cabins. Above the stateroom doors were the windows of a clerestory. These skylight windows were usually of colored glass, often sporting a multi-colored pattern, which played a dazzling ballet as the light bounced off the glass pendants of the chandeliers on to white walls. To avoid stark-white saloon and cabin interiors, some postbellum boats used walnut or rosewood inlaid with root ash and ebony panels.

The ornate cabin of side-wheeler *Katie*, 1871–1878, with the tables set for dinner. (Courtesy of S & D Reflector, from Capt. Sam G. Smith collection.)

The chandeliered cabin of the of the *Scotia*. Built in 1880. The oval inserts in the stateroom doors frame oil paintings by artist Emil Bott. (Courtesy of S & D Reflector, from Capt. Sam G. Smith collection.)

The *Gordon C. Greene*, a rather austere cabin by the standards of the day, fitted out with plain tables and chairs. The floor of polished maple in the foreground was used for evening dancing. Aft is the carpeted ladies' cabin. Note the ceiling fans. (Courtesy of S & D Reflector.)

One of the most ornate cabins along the upper Ohio in 1880 was that of the *Henry M. Stanley* with its crystal bedecked chandeliers. In this photograph each table has a centerpiece, of watermelon slices resembling water lillies in bud, each bearing fruit in its center. (Courtesy of S & D Reflector.)

Cabin of the 260-foot long stern wheel packet, *Will Kylie*, 1879–1881. Note the form of heating, a potbellied stove. (Courtesy of S & D Reflector, from Capt. Sam G. Smith collection.)

The main cabin of the *Andy Johnson*, looking aft.
Note the individual oil lamps mounted in the chandeliers. The *Andy Johnson*, a side-wheeler, was built
at St. Louis in 1865 and named after the president.
After ten years in the Keokuk Line service she was
destroyed when crushed by an ice jam at St. Louis
in December, 1876. (Courtesy of S & D Reflector.)

Cabin of the "racer" *Natchez*. This ornate cabin was
built in Cincinnati in 1869 by Elias Ealer, a noted
builder of steamboat cabins. (Courtesy of S & D Reflector, by Theo. Lilienthal & Co., from the collection
of William L. Talbot.)

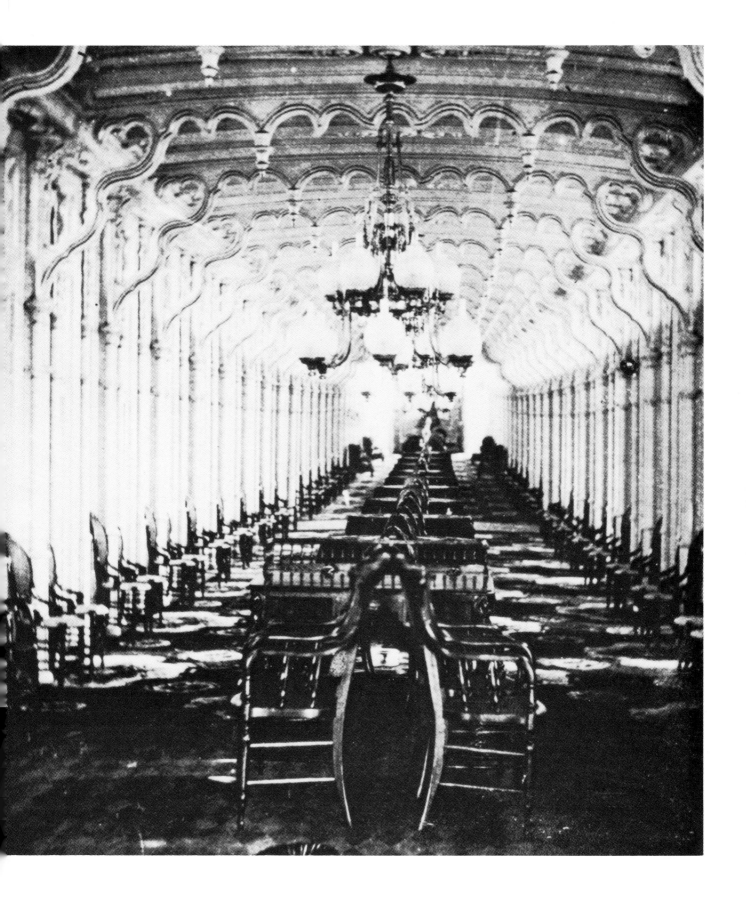

Handsome upholstered and carved furniture was often complemented by a grand piano. A large silver water cooler with drinking cups chained to its sides, was generally located at the forward end. Off to the right hand side was a bar, presenting a colorful scene of sparkling glassware, liquor bottles and mirrors. In the stern of the saloon, reserved for ladies, a huge mirror appeared to double the length of the room. Furnishings and decorations in the ladies' saloon were often more elaborate than in the men's. The most colorful aspect of the ladies' section was a bright flowered carpet, usually a Brussels, though sometimes a Wilton or a Turkish velvet. The furniture was generally of mahogany, rosewood or walnut, ornately carved and upholstered in rich fabrics such as brocade, velvet, and satin. Fine oil paintings of river scenes and symbolic sculptures decorated the saloons, adding color and elegance over the stateroom doors, the spaces above the forward entrances, the ladies' cabins and clerk's office. Many boats carried large paintings of their patron cities over the forward entrance. Statues thirty-three inches high of a Natchez chief and his squaw, carved from white pine and painted and gilded, adorned the ladies' cabin of the *Natchez* of 1869. A guilded statue of General Andrew Jackson stood in the gentlemen's cabin of the *Eclipse*. Mottoes were the rage in cabin decoration in the 1880s and 1890s and were often displayed in stained glass. "In God We Trust" shone in beautiful color in the cabins of the Lee Line boats. The cabins of the Ryman Line however, carried religious inscriptions. Hanging over the office window of the *Bob Dudley* (1897), for example, was: "Where Will You Spend Eternity." "Let Nought But Joy Possess You," "Kindness Makes Friends," and "Let Joy Abound," decorated the ladies' cabin on the *Wyoming*.

4

PADDLE STEAMER ANATOMY

The steamboat, like practically every mechanical complex of importance, was the product of many men with a common heritage of technical knowledge and equipment, all impelled by a common awareness of need. The first steamboats in the United States were built to the specification of the owners under their direction. The demonstrated success of the new vessels created a demand that led to the establishment of boatyards specializing in this new type of vessel. Specialization went a stage further when, as the market opened up, one firm would build the hull and another the machinery. The demand for increasingly ornate passenger quarters created a need for experts who in turn engaged other specialists to supply and fit furniture, utensils, and kitchen equipment. A typical boatyard was, however, a small concern, short of capital and equipment. Although thousands of steamers were built, few of the yards attained a position of more than local importance. An exception was James Rees &

Sons, Company of Pittsburgh, who became one of the foremost boat builders, producing boats for the rivers of the Americas, Africa, Europe and Asia. Some of these were made in knock-down form. James Rees & Sons provided complete economical service to the boats, including the boilers, engines, and hulls in all sizes up to three hundred feet long, mainly side- and stern-wheelers. One novel design for South America had the stern wheel recessed into the rear of the boat, and completely covered by the superstructure.

Economy was the chief selling point of the riverboat and in a catalogue published by James Rees in 1913, they claimed that their small towboats operating on the Monongahela River could transport coal for four cents a ton, compared with rail charges between the same points for forty-five cents a ton. They further claimed that from Pittsburgh to New Orleans, a distance in excess of two thousand miles, coal could be transported for less than a dollar a ton.

James Rees & Sons were builders of the first steel-hulled steamboat. Named the *Chattahooches*, she was 155 feet long, with a beam of 31 feet, and 5 feet deep. She was also the first boat in her class to have longitudinal and transverse bulkheads dividing the hull into watertight compartments. James Rees terminated their business in February 1930.

The Hull

Timber continued to be used long after steel became practical, possibly due to its capacity to absorb shock and the ease with which repairs could be carried out away from the shipyards in the main cities. The iron hull which cost twice as much as the traditional wooden one, in spite of its many advantages, was out of favor with the men in the steamboat business. They were men with limited capital who aimed for a quick return on their investments. Iron hulls never really became numerous until the end of the era. Many hulls in the early days were built with what were described variously as "double bows," "collision bulkheads," and "snag chambers." The thick heavy timbers that formed the hulls of earlier boats eventually gave way to the use of light-weight woods as far as possible. The framework and planking were usually made of white oak, but in the rest of the hull white pine, poplar

and cedar were chiefly used. Distinct features of the river steamboat were the "guards," extensions of the main deck beyond the line of the hull at the sides. The guards were adopted in the first instance on side-wheelers to protect the projecting paddle wheels from damage and to provide bracing and support for the outer ends of the paddle wheel shafts. From the widest point at the paddle wheel the guards narrowed somewhat as they approached the ends of the craft. In the fully developed steamboat they were given full rounded lines at the bow to facilitate cargo handling at the landings. The long rake at the stem made it possible for the boat to strike the mud or the sand of the sloping riverbank close enough to reach the shore by gangplanks; a slowly turning paddle wheel held this position against the current. Steamboat hulls were narrow in proportion to their length though some were built up to fifty feet wide. Twenty to thirty feet was a typical beam measurement throughout the most active decades of the steamboat era. With the dry season in mind, many steamboat hulls were designed with very light draughts, which enabled the smaller stern-wheelers (described somewhat contemptuously as the "mosquito fleet") to operate almost every day of the year. However, there were times when little cargo could be carried and the boats were restricted to passengers only. Stern-wheel propulsion was commonly used, because the propelling mechanism weighed less and stern wheels were more effective in low water than side wheels. When a hull became damaged or worn out beyond economical repair the engines were removed, refurbished and reinstalled in a new hull. The boilers were invariably scrapped. The hull was either dismantled or converted for use as a riverbank wharf boat, to assemble and load freight.

When paddle steamers required a hull inspection or repair, they were lifted out of the river broadside on marine ways. The ways were a series of parallel rail tracks running from the top of the bank, sloping down to and into the river. Cradles on wheels were mounted on the tracks. The boat was secured above these cradles which were then winched up by a steam engine through gears and chains. This process could take some considerable time since the "ways" often required a haul of 200 feet or more.

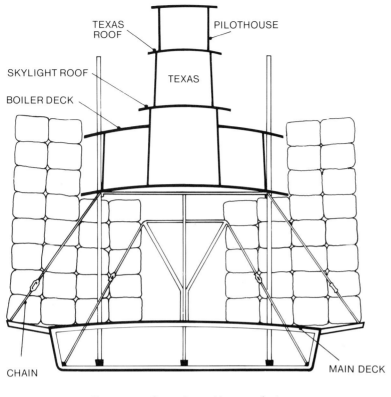

Cross section of a cotton packet

Very little freight was carried in the holds of paddle steamers. Access to the hold was through small hatches which were apt to be covered by freight. It was a dank place with little or no head room, unfit for the storage of any perishable items. Only the largest steamers used this space confining it to indestructible cargo not likely to be handled at way landings. The great bulk of packet freight was carried on the main deck, stacked in lots according to the consignee and in geographical order. Light goods could be carried almost anywhere and wintertime photos of packets are apt to show the roof covered with buggies, chairs, or chicken coops. In the summer when passenger travel was brisk these spaces were not used to such a great extent. Baled cotton was stacked on the flaring main deck of the cotton packet. The piles were carried right up past the cabin and above the roof. The drawing lists the various decks of the paddle steamer.

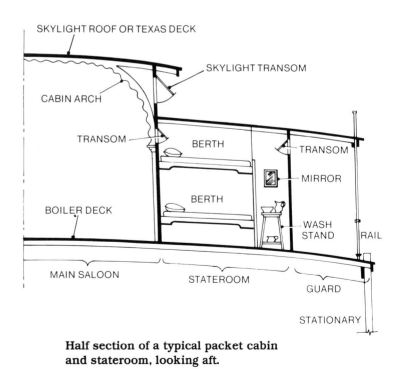

Half section of a typical packet cabin and stateroom, looking aft.

Steamer *S.S. Brown* built by James Rees & Sons
Company, Pittsburgh. Designed for the Memphis &
Vicksburgh trade, she was 228 feet long with a 44
foot beam. (Courtesy, Southern Comfort Corporation.)

Marine ways.

The *Senator Cordill*, upbound, at Wheeling, West Virginia in 1922. Note the hog chain and brace arrangement, clearly visible here. (From the collection of the Public Library of Cincinnati and Hamilton County.)

The Hog Chain System of Framing

The hull of the river paddle steamer was long and narrow. Evolved through experience, the hull gave optimum speed and improved handling characteristics when operating in shallow water. This design when applied to the wooden hull of the time, however, posed a problem. "Hogging," a tendency for the hull to arch or hog, caused by the weight and placement of machinery and cargo was an unfortunate result of the design. This condition was further aggravated by shocks to the hull when grounding, a frequent hazard. The system built into the hull and superstructure, although essential, was not apparent to the casual observer. The following is an attempt to enlighten the reader as to the extent and reasons behind this necessary but hidden system (see Figure A).

Hog chain system (A).

The hull was a very long structure in proportion to its depth. There was practically no "beam effect" to give it stiffness. Hogging was a real problem. It was solved in the 1840s with the development of the hog chain system of framing. (B) shows a stern-wheel hull in a hogged condition. (C) has the same hull with boiler, engine and paddle wheel loads applied. An unbraced hull would try to assure the shape shown and the cylinder timbers, which support the heavy paddle wheel, would droop and break. Turnbuckles on the hog chains provided adjust-ment to take up slack if bow or stern sagged. The term chains refers to wrought iron rods from one to two and one-half inches in diameter. It is easy to pull up the ends of a hull by simply hanging the ends on iron rods called chains. Wooden poles, called braces, were used to support chains. The braces were set into the recessions that ran along the bottom of the hold. Figure (D) shows a hull with this set of braces and chains. The minus signs indicate tension or pull, and the plus sign means compression or push.

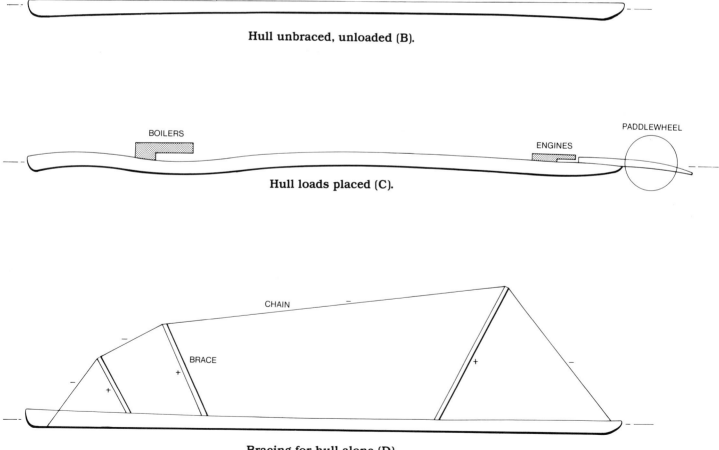

Hull unbraced, unloaded (B).

Hull loads placed (C).

Bracing for hull alone (D).

Another set of braces is needed to counteract the loads at boilers and engines. Notice how the chains pick up under these loads in (E). The engines rest on solid timber bulkheads that reach to the floors in the hull. Now add the cylinder timbers and the paddle wheel. The cylinder timbers extend from the front of the engines to the after end of the fantail and the entire structure is stiffened by braces and chains. The weight of the engines helps balance the weight of the wheel (see (E)). This is fine as long as the wheel remains at rest. When it runs however, a lot of other stresses come into being. Water is lifted and thrust back or forth. Vibrations are set up. To resist these forces wood braces are added as shown in (G). Longitudinal hogging was easier to resist in side-wheelers

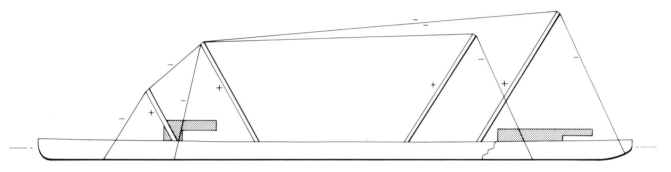

Add bracing for boilers and engines (E).

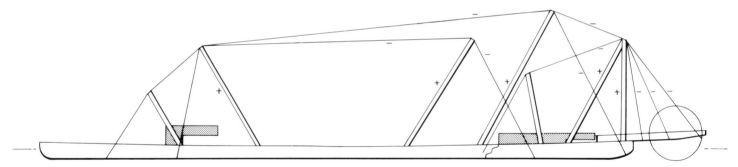

Add chains for paddle wheel (F).

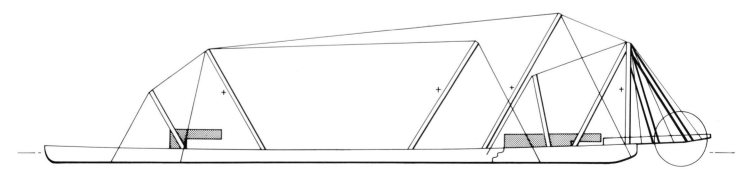

Add braces for paddle wheel complete hog chain system (G).

due to the central placement of boilers and engines. (H) shows how the ends would droop but the center would be held down by the weight of the machinery. The hog chains on most side-wheelers were kept out of sight. A few had tall systems like those in (I) but most were below the deck line. Hulls hogged laterally too, as in figure (J). This was resisted by knuckle chains which picked up the sides of the boat and pressed down on the center bulkhead. Some knuckle chains extended above deck, some did not; figure (K) gives the general idea. Cross chains carried the wide guards of cotton packets and side-wheelers. A set of them was installed at every station as shown in figure (L).

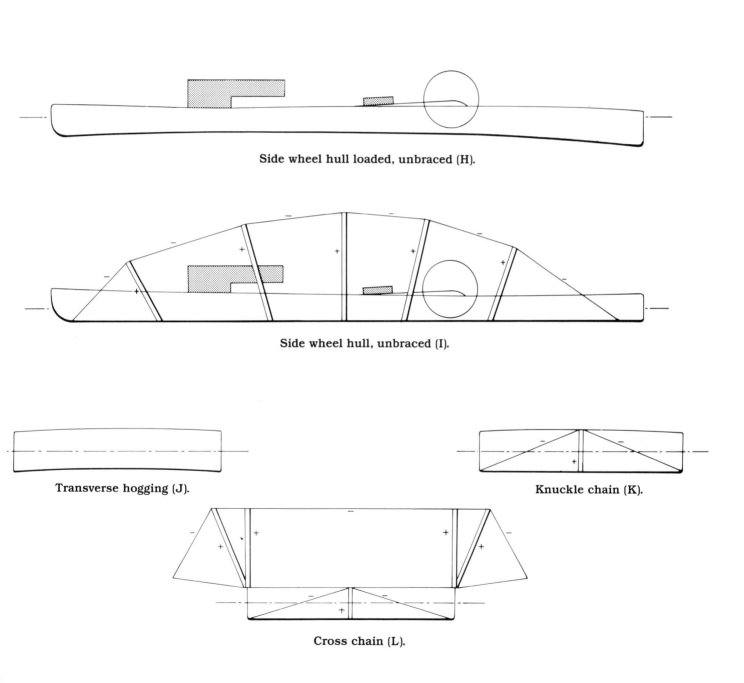

Side wheel hull loaded, unbraced (H).

Side wheel hull, unbraced (I).

Transverse hogging (J).

Knuckle chain (K).

Cross chain (L).

Engines and Boilers

The detailed progress of the paddle steamer engine is a subject in itself, but briefly the standard steamboat engine was developed from low pressure beam engines whose origination undoubtably started as stationary engines powering mills. The beam engine with its vertical cylinder gave way to the horizontal cylinder, the beam action being replaced by a direct connection between piston and crank through a connecting rod known as the "pitman." With progress in technical knowledge pressures of a hundred pounds were in common use by the year 1840. The high pressure engine had more reserve power than the earlier low pressure engine, a great asset when negotiating rapids. The horizonal cylinder was not without its problems, however. One boat builder remarked that he had

seen engines move as much as an inch at each stroke due to the working of the hull. The engines were crude in appearance and uncomplicated but they combined compactness and strength. Unlike the machinery of the traditional steamboat which presented a gleaming array of shining steel and polished brass, there was little showy about the river paddle steamer engine. What they required was low initial cost, along with easy maintenance and repair, and an abundance of power. Usually the only bright work to be seen in the engine room was in the piston rod and the throttle handle. Engines had many variations of control gear, from clumsy manual controls to complex valve arrangements relieving the steamboat engineer of the strenuous physical effort that his forebears had to suffer. The reversing gear on the original Mississippi paddle steamers, was like nothing else of its kind in the engineering world. Being of lever and poppet valve order the reversing gear was heavy.

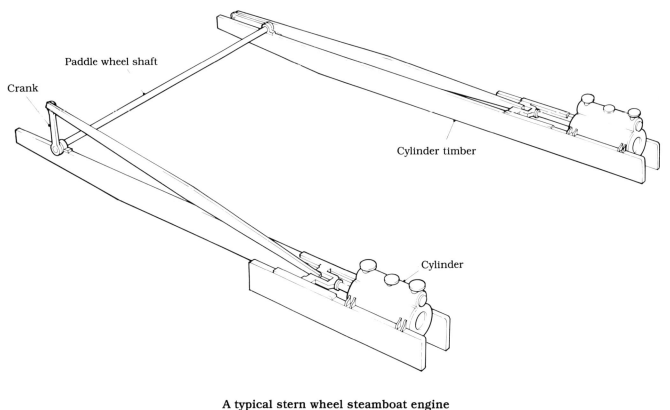

**A typical stern wheel steamboat engine
shown in its basic form without controls.**

The connecting rod, even though it was coupled to the "rock shaft" at one end, required a lift of some fifty pounds. In reversing, the other end of the connecting rod was lifted off its hook at the bottom, and a lever was thrown over which in turn raised two heavy valve levers. The rod was then lifted about three feet and dropped on the upper hook. It was a Herculean task in normal circumstances and almost impossible to do with any speed when the pilot requested it while navigating in tricky waters. At a later stage the adoption of an improved reversing gear similar to that on a railway engine enabled both engines to be operated from a single lever situated in a central position. There is no doubt that the engines, driven by both low and high pressure steam with the attendant risks did result in many unforeseen accidents. One of the many dangerous mechanical failures engineers had to face was when the boat "ran through herself"— a breakage of any of the interconnecting system commencing with the piston head and ending with the paddle wheel crank pin. Failure of any part could cause the piston to go through the piston head, resulting in great damage to the boat and injuries to the crew. Technological ignorance and lack of materials caused many such serious problems. But the engines were the most durable part of the paddle steamer. The usual practice on dismantling a steamboat was to transfer the engines to a new vessel. They were also frequently salvaged from wrecked and sunken boats. A report dated 1849 stated that "at least one-third of the new steamboats operating were equipped with old engines and machinery." It was, however, recognized as a dangerous practice to place old boilers on new steamboats, although this was sometimes done.

The steamboat boiler was second only to the engine in interest and importance. It was the most vulnerable part of the machinery and was the chief source of the paddle steamer's ill fame. Many types of boilers were tried in the early days—some upright, others horizontal; some were plain cylinders and others were fitted with internal flues. Eventually tubular boilers were introduced. Some boilers were fired from the inside and others from below. The type of boiler that was generally adopted for the riverboat was the long, horizontal cylindrical type, containing two internal flues with the firebox placed under one end. The flues usually ranged from twelve to sixteen inches in diameter. The boiler shell proper was made of wrought iron plates curved to shape and riveted together. The joints were staggered for strength. The plate thickness varied from one-sixth of an inch up to a quarter of an inch, the latter eventually adopted as standard. Due to the difficulty of giving wrought iron the required size and shape, the boiler ends were made of cast iron. The steamboat boiler in the early 1800s generally ranged from twenty-four to thirty inches in diameter and from fifteen to eighteen feet in length. By the end of the decade the measurements in common use were around forty-two inches in diameter with a length of twenty-four feet. Some of the smaller boats had only one boiler but the larger vessels with more powerful engines had as many as seven (the *Rob't E. Lee* had eight).

Over the years minor improvements in boilers and equipment increased the efficiency and reduced the hazards associated with steamboat engines. Wrought iron steam pipes replaced the original cast iron type. Cast iron had no "give" and with the springing and settling of the hull under varying conditions of load and speed, they frequently fractured, causing damage and often injury, sometimes even loss of life. Stuffing boxes and slip joints solved the problem in part; the introduction of expansion loops further reduced the risk. Wrought iron boiler heads replaced the cast iron types that were subject to cracking. The addition of a mud receiver running underneath and across the battery of boilers facilitated removal of mud and sediment, considerably reducing boiler maintenance. The mud receivers varied in diameter from twelve to eighteen inches. A steam drum placed above and across the boilers prevented water from passing into the main steam lines and cylinders, the drum diameter was twelve to twenty-four inches.

The western river-type boilers were prone to blisters on the underside of the boiler. In this state the boiler was said to be "bagged." This problem was usually confined to the crown sheet, the boiler plate directly above the furnace fire. Incrustation or sediment lodged internally prevented even dissipation of the heat, causing the affected part to bulge downward. This defect required immediate attention. One expedient was to "haul" the fire allowing the temperature to drop sufficiently and

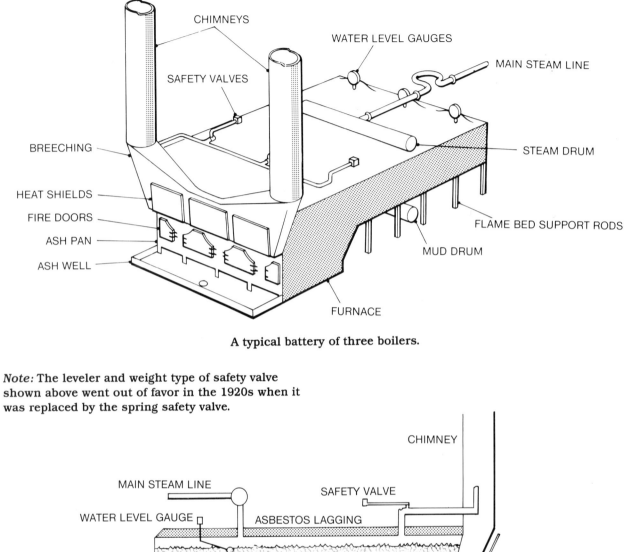

CHIMNEYS

WATER LEVEL GAUGES

MAIN STEAM LINE

SAFETY VALVES

BREECHING

STEAM DRUM

HEAT SHIELDS

FIRE DOORS

ASH PAN

FLAME BED SUPPORT RODS

ASH WELL

MUD DRUM

FURNACE

A typical battery of three boilers.

Note: The leveler and weight type of safety valve
shown above went out of favor in the 1920s when it
was replaced by the spring safety valve.

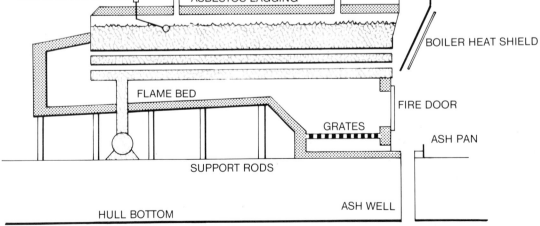

CHIMNEY

MAIN STEAM LINE

SAFETY VALVE

WATER LEVEL GAUGE

ASBESTOS LAGGING

BOILER HEAT SHIELD

FLAME BED

FIRE DOOR

GRATES

ASH PAN

SUPPORT RODS

HULL BOTTOM

ASH WELL

Section through boiler.

permit the affected area to be bricked off, protecting it from further exposure. The boat could then limp on with reduced steam pressure to the nearest boiler works. Small bulges when heated could be "driven up" to asume their original contours. Larger blisters required the replacement of the entire plate.

The introduction of new packing materials to replace the traditional red lead and canvas, rope and gasket paper, served to reduce steam loss and maintenance on glands, pipe joints and gaskets. Even the last arrival of the safety valve was not without its problems; it was almost invariably a simple poppet valve held closed by a movable weight resting on the valve beam or lever. Often poorly designed and constructed it could not be relied upon either to open at the pressure for which it was set to release, or to release steam fast enough to prevent an explosion. Sometimes the size of such valves was less than one half of that of the throttle valve. Lack of care frequently led to corrosion and sticking of the valve.

Steam gauges were slow to make their appearance on riverboats. The engineers were quite content to rely on such crude indexes of pressure as the sound and appearance of the steam issuing from the boiler water level "try cocks," when opened, or the sound of the exhaust. Experienced engineers could tell by the manner of the engine's operation what the pressure available was without reference to gauges and the like. Possibly the first gauges used were of the memory "U" type, but with the move to the high pressure engine these became impractical due to the length of tube required (a pound of steam is the equivalent in size to a two-inch column). The bourbon bent tube gauge filled this need but it was the late 1840s before it was adopted. The passing of the steamboat inspection act in 1852 made the tube compulsory.

The boilers were placed well forward to counterbalance the weight of the engines and paddle wheel aft on a stern-wheeler. Steamboat boilers were generally placed lengthwise in batteries side by side, across the forepart of the main deck. They were connected underneath by a water pipe to maintain a common level in each boiler, and their tops were joined by a steam line to the engines. The furnace end was built up with firebrick encased in sheet iron. The boilers stood free of the deck on brackets. Thus steamboat furnaces placed near the bow, with their doors facing forward had the benefit of a draught stimulated by the forward motion of the vessel. To meet the increased demand for more steam, experiments were carried out to increase this draught. One method was the injection of steam into the boiler flues. But the problem was finally resolved by increasing the height of the chimneys.

A battery of five boilers typical of the type used on steamboats. Note the steam drums mounted on and connecting with all the boilers, likewise the mud receivers mounted on the underside.

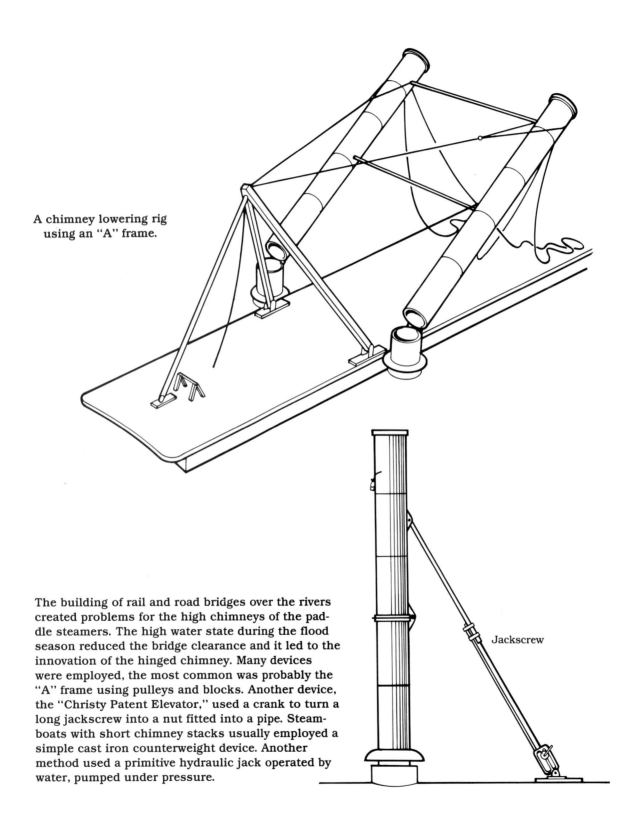

A chimney lowering rig
using an "A" frame.

The building of rail and road bridges over the rivers
created problems for the high chimneys of the paddle steamers. The high water state during the flood
season reduced the bridge clearance and it led to the
innovation of the hinged chimney. Many devices
were employed, the most common was probably the
"A" frame using pulleys and blocks. Another device,
the "Christy Patent Elevator," used a crank to turn a
long jackscrew into a nut fitted into a pipe. Steamboats with short chimney stacks usually employed a
simple cast iron counterweight device. Another
method used a primitive hydraulic jack operated by
water, pumped under pressure.

Jackscrew

In the early years of the steamboat era the chimneys (pronounced *chimleys* by the riverboat crews) rarely rose more than thirty feet above the water, and in the late 1830s fifty feet was the maximum height. Thereafter, chimney heights increased until by 1850 the tops of chimneys on the larger steamboats attained a dizzy height of ninety feet above the surface of the water. The arrival of the railroad caused bridges to be built to span the rivers. In an effort to overcome these obstructions the steamers operating in these areas had hinged chimneys. They were either counterbalanced or equipped with a specially designed lowering rig (see illustration). The great clouds of smoke and profusion of sparks belching from the chimneys and the violence of the exhaust were clear evidence of waste. Careless and ignorant management as well as poor design of the boilers were all responsible for this inefficiency. Insufficient and badly pro-

portioned grate and boiler surfaces led to the practice of driving furnaces at a furious rate, packing fuel in until the rearing firebox was fairly choked in a frantic effort to obtain sufficient steam. The lack of suitable material to insulate the cylinders, steam lines and the tops and sides of boilers allowed a large heat loss. The practice of leaving much of the lower deck exposed added further to these losses from condensation, estimated by some to be as much as fifteen percent of the fuel consumed.

The most vexatious problem connected with the control of the boilers was that of water supply. For many years the feed pump was incorporated into the engine. Although in principle automatic op-

Stern-wheeler *Joseph B. Williams* at Paducah marine ways, August 1905, after sinking at Sisters Island. Note the folding chimneys, a necessary feature. (From the collection of the Public Library of Cincinnati and Hamilton County.)

eration of the pump while the engine was in use would seem to have been more practical, in practice varying loads created a fluctuating steam requirement and created varying demands for water. Steamboats had numerous stops to make, often with frequent and extended delays at each landing. Unless care was taken to dampen the fires during stops the water level could fall and damage or weaken the boilers while mounting steam pressure would add to the danger of an explosion. An added risk on starting the engine with the pump so interconnected was the introduction of cold water into a boiler with a low water level. The shock to the boiler surfaces could result in an explosion. The fact that many boats blew up on leaving a landing would seem to support this theory. To avoid this risk the careful captain had to resort to the clumsy and wasteful practice of keeping the paddle wheels turning slowly at the landing, or moving the vessel in a circle as the passengers and cargo were taken ashore in the yawl. This serious operational defect was finally overcome by the introduction of a small auxilliary steam engine which earned the name "doctor" because it was considered a cure for the many ills of the steamboat engine.

The beams connecting the cylinder piston rod with the paddle wheel crank were called pitmans. The pitmans that connected the engines to the paddle wheel cranks were ordinarily made of pine timber reinforced with straps of iron top and bottom. To make them of cast or wrought iron was beyond the technical competence of the engineers and in any event it would have created a weight problem. Wooden pitmans did however require frequent inspection in case of shrinkage and rot, but when in good condition and properly adjusted they gave excellent service. Wooden pitmans had the ability to absorb to some degree the shocks due to the frequent sudden stoppages of the wheels on striking obstructions and so minimized the damage to the machinery. The length of the pitman was usually determined by the length of the piston stroke, but even this rule of thumb method was subject to variation as experience grew. In the late 1830s it was generally three and one-half times the sroke; in the 1860s, four times the stroke. By 1900 it had dropped back to three and three-quarters and up for the packet boats, and four and one-half to five times the stroke for towboats. Pitmans ranged

in length from twenty-four to thirty-five feet on the larger stern-wheelers. A side-wheeler with a broken pitman was a rather helpless creature. Losing the use of one wheel created difficulty in directional control and generally the steamer had to call for assistance. Some such unfortunate boats did manage to make port, but their success depended to a large extent on the position of the paddle wheel in relation to the rudders. A wing rudder positioned two-thirds over subject to paddle wheel wash could hold the vessel on course but the pilot would find himself in difficulty should any emergency arise.

The boilers of the early steamboats raised their steam by burning wood in their fireboxes. It was a clean burning fuel that had the advantage of quickly raising steam. But as steamboat traffic became heavy the lands along the rivers were cleared of the best and most accessible timber. New industry and an expanding population also made demands on timber as a fuel. Prices rose and steamboatmen became interested in obtaining a cheaper substitute. A shift to coal followed naturally and brought a rapid development of the mining industry. The type and quality of timber as a fuel varied with the location. Opinions differed as to which wood was best but it was generally accepted that oak, beech, ash and chestnut came high on the list. Cottonwood, when seasoned, burned readily enough, but did not give a lasting fire; green timber and driftwood could be used in a pinch. The lower reaches of the Mississippi afforded a resinous pine wood which in the opinion of some was the best of all steamboat fuels. Resin, lard, turpentine, oil and other highly combustible materials were occasionally used as auxiliary and emergency fuels. Many advantages came with the use of coal; the fire could be kept more uniform resulting in the generation of a greater quantity of steam; it effectively reduced the space required to store it and cut the handling costs by seventy-five per cent. But to use this fuel efficiently, modifications had to be made to the fireboxes and grates. Some engineers compromised by burning wood and coal in equal quantities producing, in their opinion, a better, hotter fire. Wood still held its own where coal was not readily available, mainly on the upper Missouri, remote from cheap coal supplies.

Another boiler-related problem was that of the quality of the water supply. In the upper reaches of the rivers the water was usually clear, but farther down it was turbid with suspended sand and silt. This mix caused heavy accumulations of mud in the boilers, lowering the efficiency of the engine by reducing the ability to raise steam, and necessitating frequent stops for boiler cleaning. One engineer on the Missouri estimated that he removed 200 tons of earth from his boilers during a twelve day trip. Later development produced the "blow out tube" and valve through which much of the mud

settling in the boiler could be ejected. This innovation along with the introduction of mud drums below the boilers greatly simplified the maintenance problem.

The Paddle Wheel

Samuel Mory of Connecticut is usually credited with the innovation of the paddle wheel. Although paddle wheels were occasionally placed within the

The paddle wheel was built around a heavy shaft; most shafts were hexagonal in shape but some were round with hexagonal upsets where the flanges fitted. The cranks were keyed to the ends of the shaft outboard of the journal. The flanges were locked on to the shaft with thin wedges called feathers. Some wheels had split flanges held together with bolts. They could be installed around the shaft without disturbing any other parts. Pockets in the flange received the wheel arms (spokes). The arms were carefully hewed to an exact fit in the arm pockets. When wet they swelled on to a tighter fit. On some wheels the arms were braced just outside the flange with cocked hats. A little further out were one or more

rows of square wooden blocks. The principal wheel bracing was at the circle just inside the bucket planks where wooden blocking was sandwiched between two wrought iron or steel circles, all thoroughly bolted together. The arms were tightened by driving wood keys between the arms and the wood circles. The end grain of the wood circles was protected by wooden gibs. The bucket planks were bolted to the arms with stirrup bolts (U bolts) run through wooden battens. Cocked hats, blocking, and keys were nailed in place but the nails were not driven home. This made them easier to pull when repairs were needed. Stern wheels were balanced by doubling the thickness of the planks opposite the cranks.

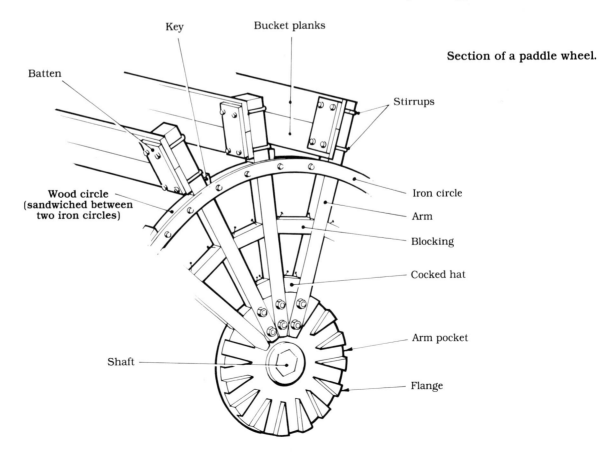

Section of a paddle wheel.

hull, chiefly on ferryboats, the customary position was at the sides or stern. Side-wheel boats predominated and remained the favorite of the river public until the end of the era, but prior to the Civil War vessels of small tonnage engaged on the tributary stream traffic were stern-wheelers. Paddle wheels spanked the water with considerable force; the resulting vibrations were felt in the most remote part of the vessel. The steamboat *Trenton* built by a Robert L. Stevens, had a paddle wheel of unique design. He made the floats or buckets in two parts, placing one above the other, and securing the upper half to the forward and the lower half to the aft side of the arm. It was said to give a smoother action, but even if it had been successful it must have had drawbacks, since it was not included in future paddle steamer designs. Experiments in Europe to increase the efficiency of the paddle wheel by altering the form or action of the buckets (paddles) were not duplicated on the American rivers. The "feathering" paddle wheel of European design was much too complicated and delicate for use on rivers which were beset with dangers such as snags, driftwood, ice, and sandbars. In the early days there were some attempts to make the paddle wheels adjustable to the varying draught by means of jacks, wedges and other devices. Nothing came of these experiments however, and in any event, with the increase in the size and weight of paddle wheels it became impractical. A measure of the weight of a typical paddle wheel was the paddle wheel shaft. On a large boat this alone could be up to fifteen inches in diameter, forty feet long, and weigh around twenty tons. Paddle wheels dominated rivers because of their ability to cope with the difficult navigational problems associated with shallow waters that were plagued with floating and fixed obstructions. When damage did occur, the wheels with only the lower section immersed were

The *Queen City*, Pittsburgh, at Wheeling, West Virginia, ca. 1908. Note the "stepped" paddle wheel. This innovation was an attempt to reduce the vibration, common to stern-wheelers, that was caused when the buckets (blades) hit the water. (From the collection of the Public Library of Cincinnati and Hamilton County.)

readily accessible and any damage to the woodwork could be easily repaired by the boat's carpenter or engineer. Thus the boat was back in service in a very short period even if damage occurred on an isolated stretch of river. Attempts were made to substitute steel for wood in paddle wheels, but the efforts proved unsatisfactory due to the need for a forge to straighten or repair the steel arms or buckets. Until it was possible to support large paddle wheels of adequate size at the stern of the steamboat, stern-wheel propulsion was of necessity confined to boats of the smallest class. Paddle wheels located at the sides of the hull not only had a more stable foundation but also supplied a needed weight midship where an excess of bouyancy was present. It also reduced hull stresses and distortion. Early stern-wheelers lacked the maneuverability of side-wheelers. In an attempt to solve this problem one

experiment involved the use of two paddle wheels side by side at the stern with independent engines, enabling the wheels to be turned in opposite directions. It gave excellent control but the weight of the additional machinery made the boat too heavy at the stern. A more successful innovation was to increase the number of rudders from two to three or even four which improved maneuverability. Improved performance was achieved by the introduction of the balanced rudder in which the blade extended beyond the rudder post and under the stern rake of the hull. This effectively increased the rudder's area and effect, and reduced the effort needed to turn since it was largely self actuating. Balanced rudders made the stern-wheeler as maneuverable as the side-wheeler and greatly accelerated the towing trade. A further unseen benefit was the even better control when going backward

The balanced rudder had about one third of its area forward of the pivot point. The pressure of the water acting on this section assisted the pilot in turning it. If the rudder was found to be too small, a "butterfly" might be added to the top to increase its area.

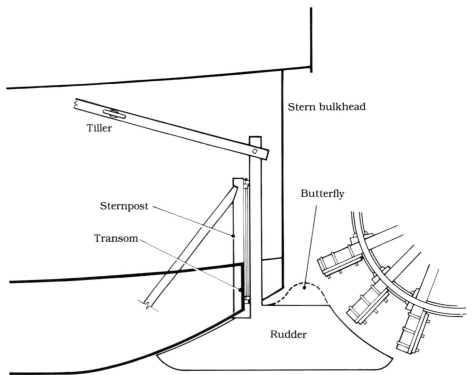

Tiller

Stern bulkhead

Butterfly

Sternpost

Transom

Rudder

enabling the boat to extract itself from some tricky navigational situations. Improvements in the design of the stern-wheeler gave it some advantages over the popular side-wheeler. The position of the paddle wheel at the stern gave it substantial protection from driftwood, logs and ice, sparing stern-wheelers much of the wear and damage to which paddle wheels and machinery were subject to on side-wheelers. The stern-wheeler was able to operate on narrow streams, in shallow water and during the low-water periods when her larger sisters were laid up. With the paddle wheels removed from the sides and the guards eliminated, the hull could be given a wider beam and consequently a more shallow draught than that of a side-wheel vessel of the same tonnage class. This consideration was of some importance. It gave the stern-wheeler the ability to carry more cargo and operate over a longer season. The position of the wheel at the stern was useful in getting the boat off bars and over shoals. It also had the advantage of avoiding the wide variation of paddle wheel "dip" by varying the forward positioning of the load to give optimum immersion of the stern and paddle wheel. Unable to compete with the advancing railways in speed, the need for fast, showy boats declined and economy of construction and operation became paramount. The stern-wheeler, cheaper to build and run, with a lighter draught and greater cargo capacity, steadily replaced the more elegant and speedier side-wheeler. Although toward the end of the era, the stern-wheelers were chiefly employed in the towing trade the steam towboat finally became extinct with the withdrawal of the Mississippi *Lone Star* in 1967.

Frequent breakage of paddle wheel shafts and cranks added to the engineers problems. The limits imposed by the foundry trip hammers of the day meant that they could not be given the required size and strength. It was necessary to resort to shafts made by casting, some of which did in fact give excellent service. Henry Clay, writing of his experiences on a trip down the Mississippi in 1819 remarked, "We passed on the Mississippi two, if not three, steam boats, which were lying by, having broken their cranks; such accidents are frequent. Indeed I doubt whether any boat, that has been a year or two on these waters, has escaped them. When they occur, the boat is subject to a detention of from thirty to fifty days, depending on the distance where the accident occurs from Louisville, to which place resort is usually had to supply the loss."

The Bells

Paddle steamers had four speeds ahead and four backward (astern). The normal cruising speed in either direction was known as full ahead, the setting below this was known as half head or half speed, and lower still was dead slow. The fastest and most powerful speed was full stroking when steam was fed into the cylinders for the entire length of the stroke with the throttle wide open. The pilot communicated his requirements to the engineer by a system of wire activated bells. They were located overhead in the engine room, three were suspended on spiral springs so that when they were activated they sprung back and forth jingling several times. Most boats used four bells, the largest and deepest in tone was the "stopping bell." Slightly smaller and next in line was the "backing bell." The next bell was in fact a gong rung by operating a clapper. It rang once each time the wire was pulled

A signal bell, one of the various types to be found in the paddle steamer's engine room. Operated by wire from the pilot house, it signalled the pilot's instructions to the engineer. This bell was also referred to as the "gong" or "ship up bell." The code of bells, although fully understood by the engineer, was usually beyond the comprehension of the layman.

and was known as the "ship up gong." The fourth in this line of bells was the baby of the three spirally mounted bells and known as the "jingle bell," or "chestnut bell." This bell system of passing orders to the engineer was usually beyond the understanding of landsmen. The following are various signals:

To call the Engineer to his post before starting anything:
Ring 3 or 4 gongs.

To come ahead:
Ring the stopping bell.

To stop from either direction:
Ring the stopping bell.

Half head in either direction:
Ring one gong after establishing the direction with either the stopping, or backing bell.

Dead slow in either direction:
Ring one gong and the jingle after establishing the direction with either the stopping or the backing bell.

From half hand to full head, either direction:
Ring one gong.

From half head to dead slow, either direction:
Ring the jingle bell.

From dead slow to half head either direction:
Ring the jingle bell.

From dead slow to full head, either direction:
Ring the jingle ell and then the gong.

Full stroke, either direction:
Ring the gong twice.

To ship up the engines from ahead to back or from back to ahead, when the engines are stopped:
Ring one gong.

Finished with engines:
Ring 3 or 4 gongs.

A big roof bell was an essential part of the boat's equipment. It was often a work of art in both tone and decoration, and was the voice by which the boat was known along the rivers. It was a frequent practice to toss two or three hundred silver dollars into the metal before pouring to insure a silvery tone. Bells usually outlived their boats and a fine specimen could be salvaged and serve on a succession of boats. Many found their way into church belfries.

In the main this old time baling wire and bell arrangement was reliable but the occasional broken wire or jammed pulley resulted in a few anxious moments. With this manual system engineers not only interpreted the pilot's wishes, but could tell who was on watch. The speaking tube was added to pass on instructions outside the scope of the bell code. In a boat in a Louisville trade, an elephant was being transported in the deckroom. It got to exploring overhead with its trunk and jingled the wires creating a confused set of signals to the engineer. Luckily the pilot also heard the ringing through his return tube trumpet in the pilot house, and a potential disaster was avoided. But the disadvantages of the system were illustrated well by this incident.

5

PADDLE STEAMER CREWS

The reputation of a passenger boat depended greatly upon the esteem in which the captain, clerks and pilots were held by the traveling public. In this respect the personality was paramount. The captain, unlike his sea-going counterpart was generally more of an owner/manager who left the navigation and operation of the boat to the pilot and the mate. Anyone with enough money to purchase a majority interest in a steamboat might set himself up as a captain. No master's license or certificate of rating was required. He in fact, was the manager of a business enterprise, but, once having left port he became the legal authority over the passengers and crew. It was the practice at the end of a voyage, where, in the opinion of the passengers, the captain and his crew had performed services above and beyond the call of duty, to give a written commendation recording the fact. This could refer to a gallant action in an emergency, or extra special service by the crew during the voyage. Needless to say, such commendations were highly prized. Many, if not most of the captains owned interests in the boats which they commanded. Some were sole owners, in which case they were answerable to no one except the civil authorities in case of legal technicalities, and to the unwritten laws of the service, which custom had made binding upon all. Such for instance, was the rule that the captain would not interfere with the pilot in navigating the boat.

The captain typically was a man with some years of practical experience on the river in one capacity or another. He usually had served as a pilot, mate or engineer, and would have valuable experience in most aspects of steamboat operation. In small steamers he often had a double role as captain and pilot, or mate. The captain's domain was in the forward part of the texas where a commodious and handsomely furnished cabin served as office, sitting room and occasionally dining room where fa-

Steamboat pilot's license, May, 1926.

C Form 874   File No. L 697

SERIAL NUMBER   ISSUE NUMBER
30951   ~ 2 , 2 ~

UNITED STATES DEPARTMENT OF COMMERCE
STEAMBOAT INSPECTION SERVICE

LICENSE TO FIRST-CLASS PILOT OF STEAM VESSELS

This is to certify that Joe Bentley Neale having given satisfactory evidence to the undersigned United States Local Inspectors, Steamboat Inspection Service, for the district of Louisville, Kentucky, that he is trustworthy and faithful, and possesses the requisite knowledge and skill, is hereby licensed to act as First-Class Pilot on Steam Vessels of not over 250 gross tons, upon the waters of the Ohio River between Owensboro, Kentucky and Cannelton, Ind.

for the term of five years from this date.
Given under our hands this 5th day of May, 1926.

Eduard Maurer
U.S. Local Inspector of Hulls.

Isaac W. Betts
U.S. Local Inspector of Boilers.

O Form 419

Steamboat pilot's license
for the Ohio and Kentucky rivers, June, 1913.

vored guests were invited to dine. It connected with
a sleeping compartment, larger and better furnished than the ordinary passenger staterooms.
From his sitting room windows he could observe
everything that was going on both aboard and
ashore. From his berth directly under the pilot
house, he could interpret the actions of the man
on watch from the sounds of his shuffling feet and
of the bell pulls, and he could thus determine the
location of the boat. The pilot, unlike his sea-going
counterpart, spent the whole of his watch in the
pilot house atop the boat. He was regarded as the
most important man aboard, and his license depended upon his total and absolute knowledge of
the river upon which he operated. He had complete
authority in deciding the boat's movements, and
his decisions were always final. The safety of the
boat was in his hands at all times. His skills included the ability to know where he was at any
time of day or night. In adverse conditions with
poor visibility, he would, by using memorized silhouettes, sound echoes from hills and buildings
to relate his position. He had to read the river's
surface to note any under water changes and except for straight stretches where he might hand
over the wheel to a trainee cub pilot, he never left
his six-hour watch. A knowledgeable pilot could
also read the language of the scape pipes, which
would tell him of conditions below decks where the
engineer wrestled with the primitive controls. To
the tuned senses of the pilot, there were also subtly
perceptible changes in the operation of the engine
and speed of the boat as it passed from one depth
of water to another. Due to the different river beds
and varying water volume at peak periods, rivers
were wont to change their course many times. It
was only the skill of the pilots in recognizing these
changes that minimized the number of riverboat
accidents. Pilots, ever aware of the danger and delay caused by reefs, had to be familiar with the
variations upon the more common flat ledge on the

An example of today's comprehensive charts, issued
by the United States Army Corps of Engineers for
the Ohio River, January, 1979. (See page 83 for
clearance data on bridges and aerial crossings.)
(Courtesy of the United States Army Corps of Engineers.)

1829 GENERAL ANDREW JAC
arrived at Cincinnati by stea
from Louisville — on his w
Washington to assume the
dency — The newspapers re
that: "The noble steamboat
conveyed him was flanked or
side by one of nearly equal si
splendor; the roofs of all thre
covered by a crowd of men; c
saluted them from the shore."

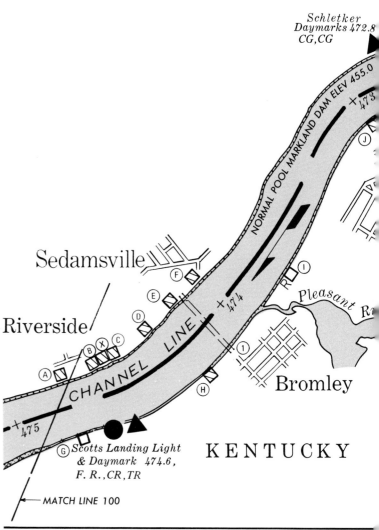

Schletker
Daymarks 472.8
CG,CG

NORMAL POOL MARKLAND DAM ELEV 455.0

+473

J

Sedamsville

F

E

D

Riverside

B X C

A

CHANNEL LINE

+474

I

Pleasant R

I

Bromley

H

+475

KENTUCKY

G *Scotts Landing Light*
& Daymark 474.6,
F. R., CR, TR

← MATCH LINE 100

RMY ENGINEER DISTRICT, LOUISVILLE

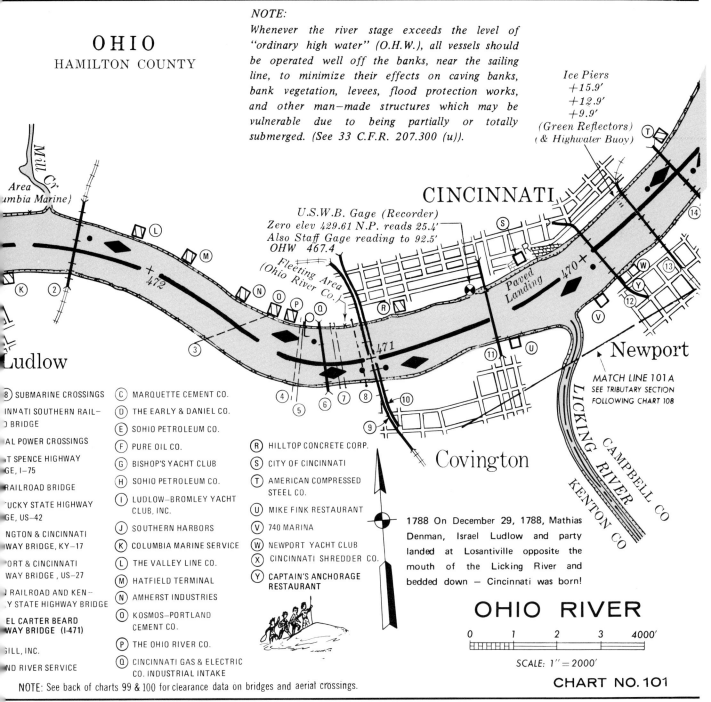

OHIO
HAMILTON COUNTY

NOTE:
Whenever the river stage exceeds the level of "ordinary high water" (O.H.W.), all vessels should be operated well off the banks, near the sailing line, to minimize their effects on caving banks, bank vegetation, levees, flood protection works, and other man—made structures which may be vulnerable due to being partially or totally submerged. (See 33 C.F.R. 207.300 (u)).

Ice Piers
+15.9'
+12.9'
+9.9'
(Green Reflectors)
(& Highwater Buoy)

Mill Cr.

Area
umbia Marine)

CINCINNATI

U.S.W.B. Gage (Recorder)
Zero elev 429.61 N.P. reads 25.4'
Also Staff Gage reading to 92.5'
OHW 467.4

Fleeting Area
(Ohio River Co.)

Paved Landing

470+

+472

471

Newport

Ludlow

MATCH LINE 101 A
SEE TRIBUTARY SECTION
FOLLOWING CHART 108

LICKING RIVER
CAMPBELL CO
KENTON CO

8 SUBMARINE CROSSINGS

INNATI SOUTHERN RAIL–
BRIDGE

AL POWER CROSSINGS

T SPENCE HIGHWAY
GE, I–75

RAILROAD BRIDGE

UCKY STATE HIGHWAY
GE, US–42

NGTON & CINCINNATI
WAY BRIDGE, KY–17

ORT & CINCINNATI
WAY BRIDGE , US–27

RAILROAD AND KEN–
Y STATE HIGHWAY BRIDGE

EL CARTER BEARD
WAY BRIDGE (I-471)

ILL, INC.

ND RIVER SERVICE

C MARQUETTE CEMENT CO.
D THE EARLY & DANIEL CO.
E SOHIO PETROLEUM CO.
F PURE OIL CO.
G BISHOP'S YACHT CLUB
H SOHIO PETROLEUM CO.
I LUDLOW–BROMLEY YACHT CLUB, INC.
J SOUTHERN HARBORS
K COLUMBIA MARINE SERVICE
L THE VALLEY LINE CO.
M HATFIELD TERMINAL
N AMHERST INDUSTRIES
O KOSMOS–PORTLAND CEMENT CO.
P THE OHIO RIVER CO.
Q CINCINNATI GAS & ELECTRIC CO. INDUSTRIAL INTAKE

R HILLTOP CONCRETE CORP.
S CITY OF CINCINNATI
T AMERICAN COMPRESSED STEEL CO.
U MIKE FINK RESTAURANT
V 740 MARINA
W NEWPORT YACHT CLUB
X CINCINNATI SHREDDER CO.
Y CAPTAIN'S ANCHORAGE RESTAURANT

Covington

1788 On December 29, 1788, Mathias Denman, Israel Ludlow and party landed at Losantiville opposite the mouth of the Licking River and bedded down — Cincinnati was born!

OHIO RIVER

0 1 2 3 4000'

SCALE: 1" = 2000'

CHART NO. 101

NOTE: See back of charts 99 & 100 for clearance data on bridges and aerial crossings.

river bottom. A rainbow reef was arched-shaped, a fish-basket reef was circular, causing tremendous difficulties. To jump a reef was to go downbound, with the current, over it; to mount a reef was to climb over it (upbound). To break a reef was to send explorer waves ahead to shape it into sight by stopping the boat short of where the pilot suspected or knew the reef to be and letting waves from the boat run up to it. The break in the reef was the gateway through it. Much of the vaunted ability of old time pilots to read the water was concerned with calculating reefs. He also had to avoid becoming "saddlebagged," or wrapped around an immovable object. This occurred when the boat hit something broadside, or got caught on a ridge on a falling river. In navigating the rivers, vessels proceeding downstream usually kept to the main channel and to the outside of the bends where the depth of water and swift current was to their advantage. Going upstream they hugged the more shallow but relatively slack water along the inside of the bends, frequently crossing the main channel in the process. A flood stage on the rivers enabled a skilled pilot to cut down the distance and time of the boat's journey by taking cut-offs at islands, and short cuts across fields to avoid the full force of the current. In the golden age of steamboats, some enthusiasts quoted a figure of over 16,000 miles of navigable rivers, but these included narrow and shallow waterways not always commercially viable except in flood conditions. The characteristically winding rivers were rarely the most direct routes. From time to time, stretches of water would have to be closed due to ice or shallow water. Up-to-date knowledge of the changing situation was therefore essential to the river pilot. To know upstream and downstream was in effect having to be knowledgeable of two rivers; when the boat is heading upstream all the indications are reversed from downstream, giving a different pattern of marks to

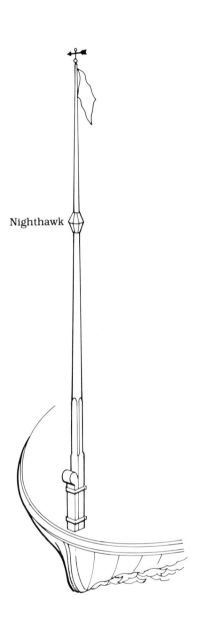

Nighthawk

The jackstaff, located on the bow of a paddle steamer, was more than a flagpole put there just to support the "navy Jack." It was a navigation aid which enabled the pilot to judge the boat's position and direction. it also supported a bulbous device, usually brightly colored, called a "nighthawk." The nighthawk when adjusted to a point level with the pilot's eyes, helped him gauge heights and distances. it was also an invaluable aid for ascertaining indistinct shorelines at night.

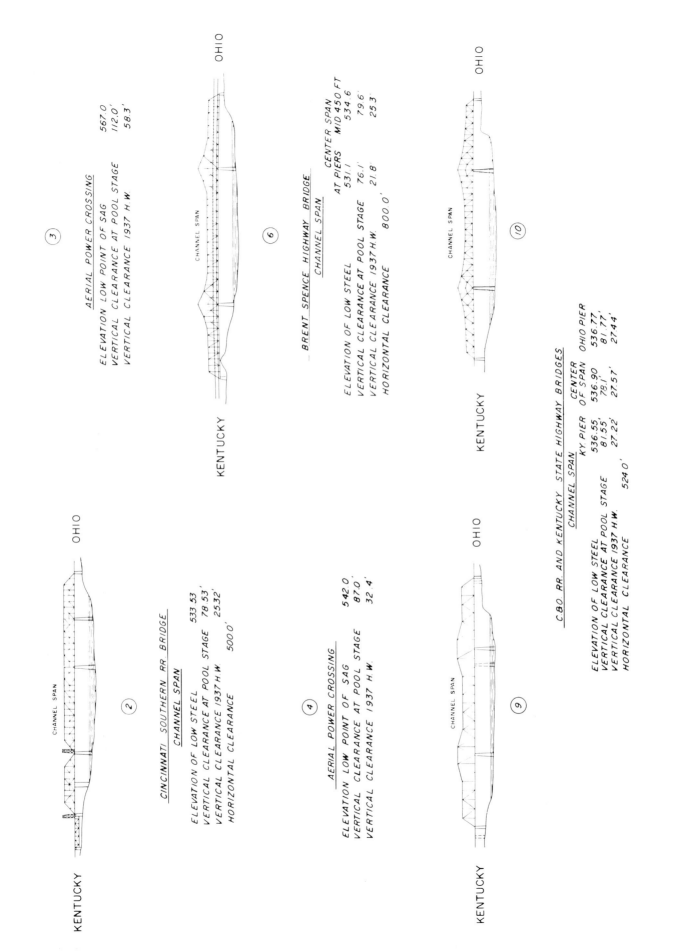

OHIO

AERIAL POWER CROSSING

ELEVATION LOW POINT OF SAG	567.0
VERTICAL CLEARANCE AT POOL STAGE	112.0'
VERTICAL CLEARANCE 1937 H.W.	58.3'

(3)

KENTUCKY

CHANNEL SPAN

(6)

BRENT SPENCE HIGHWAY BRIDGE
CHANNEL SPAN

	CENTER SPAN	
	AT PIERS	MID 450 FT
ELEVATION OF LOW STEEL	531.1	534.6
VERTICAL CLEARANCE AT POOL STAGE	76.1'	79.6'
VERTICAL CLEARANCE 1937 H.W.	21.8	25.3'
HORIZONTAL CLEARANCE	800.0'	

OHIO

CHANNEL SPAN

(10)

KENTUCKY

KENTUCKY

CHANNEL SPAN

(2)

CINCINNATI SOUTHERN RR BRIDGE
CHANNEL SPAN

ELEVATION OF LOW STEEL	533.53
VERTICAL CLEARANCE AT POOL STAGE	78.53'
VERTICAL CLEARANCE 1937 H.W.	25.32'
HORIZONTAL CLEARANCE	500.0'

OHIO

AERIAL POWER CROSSING

ELEVATION LOW POINT OF SAG	542.0
VERTICAL CLEARANCE AT POOL STAGE	87.0'
VERTICAL CLEARANCE 1937 H.W.	32.4'

(4)

OHIO

CHANNEL SPAN

(9)

KENTUCKY

C.B.O. RR. AND KENTUCKY STATE HIGHWAY BRIDGES
CHANNEL SPAN

	KY. PIER	CENTER OF SPAN	OHIO PIER
ELEVATION OF LOW STEEL	536.55	536.90	536.77
VERTICAL CLEARANCE AT POOL STAGE	81.55'	78.1'	81.77'
VERTICAL CLEARANCE 1937 H.W.	27.22	27.57	27.44
HORIZONTAL CLEARANCE	524.0'		

read. In later years the provision of locks and canals to by-pass rapids, eased the pilot's task. However, the provision of such works was bedevilled by politics both local and national, and debates over who should bear the cost. The problem was resolved in the mid-eighties, with the formation of a civilian corps of engineers to construct works and maintain rivers.

The pilot had to decide when to stop his journey to seek shelter—he had to respect the river and its power. To illustrate such power, there is a story of a steamboat seeking shelter on the Missouri during a bad storm. The pilot ordered the boat to be moored to a tree thirty yards from the bank. So swiftly did the fast flowing current eat into the bank, however, that within half an hour the tree was undermined and the pilot had to repeat the process upstream.

Another illustration of the erosive power of water can best be related in a story of the steamboat *America*. In 1836 at Plum Point on the Mississippi below Cairo the *America* sank close to the Arkansas shore. A few years later the position of the main channel shifted until it passed between the wreck and shore. The wreck then formed a core about which an island was born. Trees grew on this island, were cut down, and a house was built and cornfield planted. Some years passed and the situation was reversed—the farm and island were swept away and the river resumed its original course. In 1865, salvagers found the wreck in forty feet of water and succeeded in not only recovering a valuable cargo of lead, but engines and boilers as well.

Eventually, the pilots formed an association and organized locked boxes at intervals along the rivers. They posted up-to-date reports on river conditions in these boxes for perusal by their fellow members. A rather tardy measure to assist navigation and improve safety, was the provision of beacon lights and mile posts along the river banks in the 1870s. Today the United States coast guard advises pilots of river conditions by bulletin and radio.

Pilots were highly skilled and responsible men, and it is easy to understand why they were held in awe, and indeed, why some often acquired legendary stature. However the endless stream of accidents from causes avoidable by the man at the wheel would indicate that they were by no means a race of supermen.

Of all the officers, the mate was closest in spirit to the flatboat era with its emphasis on brawn, violence and abusive language. The mate was the captain's deputy and his duties were manifold. He supervised the deck hands and any man-handling of the boat. He was responsible for cargo handling, not such a simple task since weight distribution was an important factor. Both speed and economy were affected by the manner in which he applied his skills to this important part of his duties. The cargo had to be positioned so that it was accessible at the many points of discharge. Cargo also had to be categorized, certain types either not allowed aboard, or not to be mixed with others. All this information was later laid down in a manual, but the mate had to know it by heart. He also had to be available to assist the captain and pilot at all times, and to handle any untoward situation that might arise during the voyage. His authority extended over the deck crew who generally comprised about half the entire crew. Mostly casual workers, their lot was a degrading one, they bore the brunt of the hardship and dangers of steamboat life. A few gunny sacks, a bit of straw, a ragged blanket or old overcoat served as a hand's bedding. In the early steamboat years, they were recruited from the older established classes of boatmen on the rivers. They were, proverbially, a rough, dissolute and often lawless lot, both feared and shunned by the citizens of the river towns because of their rowdy and riotous behavior. On July 29, 1869 a riot aboard the sidewheeler *Dubuque*, instigated by drunk raftsmen, resulted in the deaths of six Negro crew members who tried to restore order. It was not unknown for the owners of slaves to hire them out to steamboat captains as deck hands. This created problems when the boat went into Northern free territory, many vessels dropped off the deck crew slaves in Kentucky replacing them with white labor. Discipline of the hands was rough and ready. At the slightest provocation they were beaten, knocked down, clubbed and at times were even stabbed, shot or thrown overboard.

Steamboat mate's license issued in April, 1909.

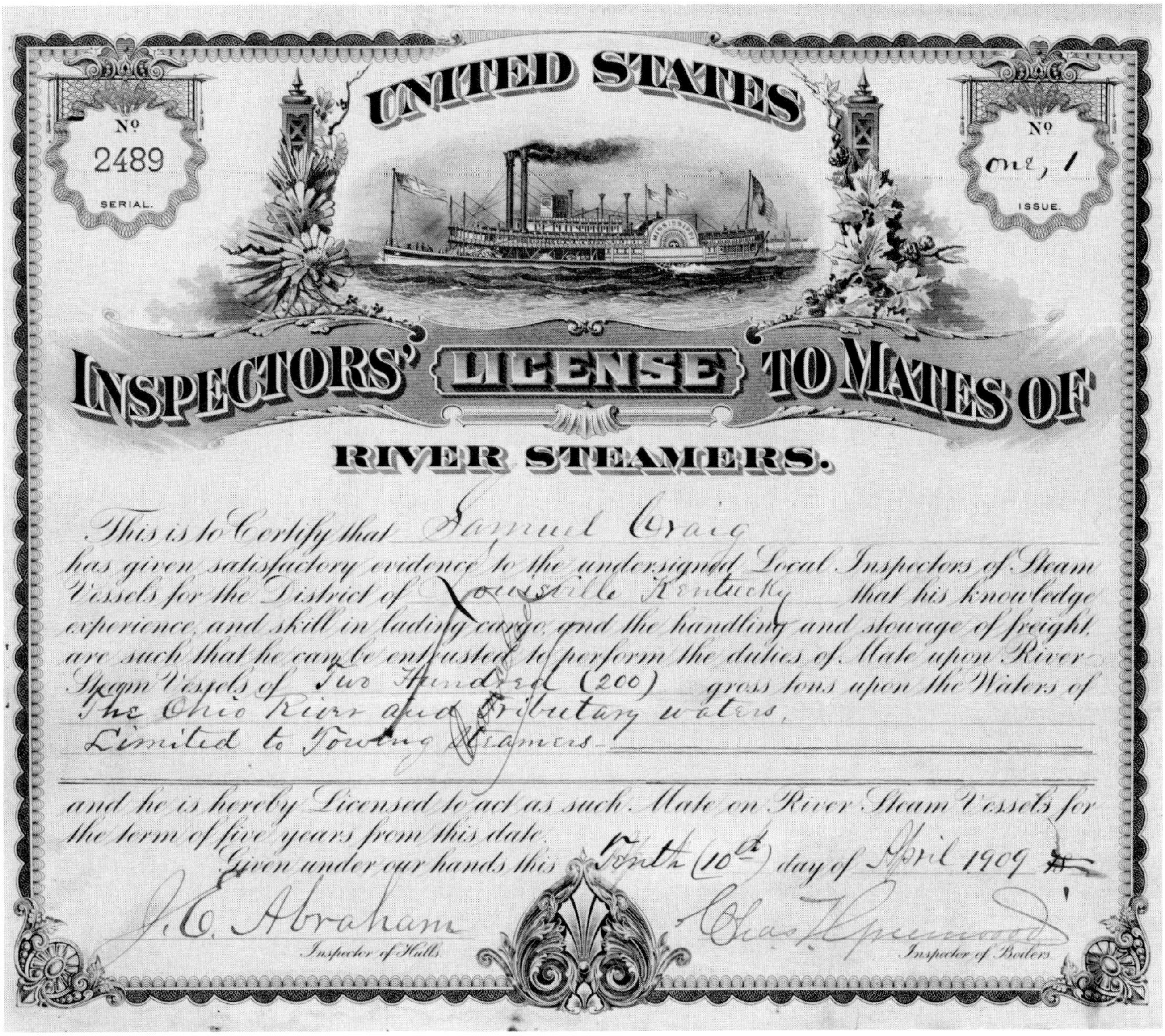

No 2489 SERIAL.

No One, 1 ISSUE.

UNITED STATES

INSPECTORS' LICENSE TO MATES OF RIVER STEAMERS.

This is to Certify that Samuel Craig has given satisfactory evidence to the undersigned Local Inspectors of Steam Vessels for the District of Louisville Kentucky that his knowledge experience, and skill in lading cargo, and the handling and stowage of freight are such that he can be entrusted to perform the duties of Mate upon River Steam Vessels of Two Hundred (200) gross tons upon the Waters of The Ohio River and tributary waters, Limited to Towing Steamers-

and he is hereby Licensed to act as such Mate on River Steam Vessels for the term of five years from this date.

Given under our hands this Tenth (10th) day of April 1909

J. C. Abraham
Inspector of Hulls.

Chas. H. Greenwood
Inspector of Boilers.

Steamboat engineer's license, October, 1918.

C. & L. Form 876   File No. L 1037

SERIAL NUMBER   ISSUE NUMBER
58786   4-4

DEPARTMENT OF COMMERCE AND LABOR
STEAMBOAT INSPECTION SERVICE
UNITED STATES
LICENSE
TO
CHIEF ENGINEER OF STEAM VESSELS

This is to certify that *George A. McNeece*, having been duly examined by the undersigned United States Local Inspectors, Steamboat Inspection Service, for the district of *Evansville   Ind.*, as to his knowledge of steam machinery and as to his experience, and found to be competent, is hereby licensed to act as Chief Engineer on *non* condensing *River* steam vessels of *any* gross tons, for the term of five years from this date.

Given under our hands this *28* day of *Oct.*, 19*18*

R. H. Williams
U.S. Local Inspector of Hulls.

Baylor Shratt
U.S. Local Inspector of Boilers.

Engineers in general had to be trained from scratch since none had previously existed, thus they were in short supply for years. The employment of engineers was often "Hobson's Choice." Consequently, breakdowns and disasters were more frequent than they should have been. Apprentice engineers (stikers or cub engineers) began their training by oiling and cleaning machinery and tending the boilers. To give the engineer credit, one must remember that once the boat was commissioned, the time for proper maintenance was limited, and the machinery would be literally worked to death in most cases. Save for brief landings on the long distance runs, engines operated twenty-four hours a day, leaving little opportunity to make necessary adjustments and repairs. Working in the engine rom, which was invariably hot, the engineer was at the beck and call of the pilot. He had to be alert constantly, in case the latter signalled that a change of speed or direction was necessary. When a given signal was received, there was no time to lose since the safety of the boat would be at stake. Engineering science being in its infancy and the ever present possibility of a boiler explosion, a fractured cylinder head, or burst steam pipes added to the engineer's misery.

Descaling the boilers was one of the less attractive tasks of a cub engineer that was carried out between trips. As soon as the boat was made fast the "mud valves" were opened, the fires drawn, the water released from the boilers, then the process of cleaning began. Entering the boiler shell through a manhole, thus equipped with a hammer and a sharp-linked chain, the apprentice chipped away at the hard scale by pounding it with the hammer, and by using the chain with a sawing motion he cleaned around the flues. The loose mud and sediment was then flushed out by a stream of water from a hose, connected to a hand-operated force pump. Some of the earlier boats carried a regular blacksmith's forge, and the boat's engineer, in addition to his other skills, needed to be experienced in the blacksmithing. Many running repairs were made using parts forged on the anvil from wrought-iron bars: the bucket stirrups (U bolts), hog chains and chimney guys to name but a few.

Forward on the boiler deck, and adjoining the main saloon opposite the bar was the office. This was the domain of the steamboat clerk or purser.

A roustabout, the lowest form of humanity in the steamboat deck crew, was usually portrayed as a Negro although most of them were white men from flatboat or keelboat crews. Around 1840, the majority of roustabouts were Irish or German immigrants. They were on duty twenty-four hours a day, seven days a week. Their food consisted of leftovers from the tables of the cabin passengers, and mealtime was a free for all, with each man clawing into the various pans, grabbing food: meat remnants in one pan, bread and cakes in another, and jellies and custards in a third.

There were no living quarters for the roustabouts. When not working, they curled up on cotton bales or in between cargo, with old overcoats or gunny sacks for bedding. Their work was always heavy, often dangerous, poorly paid, and without dignity.

His duties as chief clerk were numerous and included issuing tickets for passage and staterooms, showing passengers around the boat, answering a multitude of questions, and in many ways making the voyage an agreeable experience for them. His main occupation was that of logging and charging out for the cargo as it moved on and off the boat. His office accommodated a mail rack also. Another title bestowed on him or his subordinate was "mud clerk." This nickname was earned by standing knee deep in mud at the end of the landing stage, counting passengers, chickens, pigs, crates and bales or whatever cargo moved on or off the boat.

Of all the positions in a crew, the cabin crew was the least interesting. These workers were little more than hotel staff transferred to the river. They included cooks, stewards, waiters, cabin boys and chambermaids. Their wages, with the possible exception of the first cook and first steward were below that of the deck crew, but their working conditions were somewhat better as they enjoyed the shelter and comfort of the passenger areas. They invariably managed to fare better with regard to food also, dining on leftovers. On the riverboat the crew ate in regulation style at the officers' table, located forward of any other tables set for passengers. The captain, instead of sitting with a select group of passengers, was king at the officers' table. He sat at the head, facing aft surveying the whole cabin. On his right would be the pilot and on the left the chief engineer, and so on with the rest of the crew taking up their recognized and jealously guarded positions. Steamboat crews varied in number, from the four or five hands on the smaller boats, up to the 121 man crew required to operate the 1,100 ton eclipse.

6

Five to seven miles an hour (rivermen rarely talked in knots) was a fair port-to-port upstream speed for most vessels. Fifty miles a day upstream by some of the early steamers was a matter for congratulation, but by 1825 they traveled as much as one hundred miles. Judged by twentieth-century standards these speeds are far from impressive, but to a generation which had been dependent on the stagecoach and keelboat the steamboats had revolutionary consequences. Within a few years, villages grew into cities, and the whole course of commerce changed.

In the early to middle period of the riverboats reign, the average life of such craft was only three to four years, due to many mishaps and accidents such as obstructions, frequent groundings at low water, sand bars, as well as rot and deterioration from exposure to sun and air when stranded or beached during the low water season took their toll. Also the powerful engines often operated at excessive pressures, causing explosions and fires, and the strain of direct landings on unsuitable river banks shortened the boat's life span. It seems that the riverboats' fragility was related to cost and quick return on the limited capital available. Of the 178 steamboats running in 1829, only eighteen were more than four years old, and just four had been in operation more than six years; none had reached the age of ten. Daily progress in design made existing boats less and less competitive. New boats were larger and faster, capable of maintaining speeds of up to fifteen miles per hour. These naturally gave a speedier service, and in consequence, more frequent and longer voyages could produce a better return on investment. This was true for the greater part of the year, but as the levels dropped in the low water season and the rivers became narrower, the larger boats were laid up and the smaller craft came back into their own. A prolonged low water season would finally force the large boats to be tied up in port. George Fitch in his classic essay, declared that a steamboat "must be so built that when the river is low and the sand bars come out for air the first mate can tap a keg of beer and run the boat for four miles on the suds." It would seem, that, depending on which river the steamboat operated, a typical season could last from three months to a year. A full season depended on the whim of the weather. Floods, drought and ice were the ruling factors, and when the boats were laid up, some crew members reverted to their original calling of farming, an asset in lean times.

In the mid-1800s, wood fuelled the steamboats, and the steam raising qualities varied widely between pine knots and cottonwood, green timber and driftwood. Sometimes it was necessary to refuel twice a day. This provided employment for many riverside dwellers as wood yard men, and to the establishment of wood yards, where flatboats were loaded up and, in some cases, towed alongside the steamboat on its way upstream. There the wood was unloaded, and the flatboats were released and drifted back to the wood yard. (Flatboats were rarely towed downstream because there was no way for them to return except by paying for a tow.) The greatest danger in the transaction was that larger packets, or passenger boats, might swamp the flatboat by running at too great a speed, towing her under by the head. To avoid this, the wood was always taken first from the front of the flat boat.

The packets were not in so much of a hurry when going downriver, for then they had fewer passengers to feed and no fast freight.

Before flatboats were used, steamboats carried oxen to haul wood to the boat side, and sawmills on board cut timber as the boat proceeded. A measure of the scale of the wood trade was the fact that this commodity absorbed about a third of the running costs. Riverbank farmers also supplemented their incomes by cutting wood for steamboats. Notices were displayed on the stacks left near the riverbank requesting the captains to leave cash in payment. Wood from abandoned fur company stockades also found its way into the ever hungry fireboxes of the steamers. A combination of the introduction of coal in plenty and the dearth of local wood supplies, plus the decline of the steamboat, saw the end of this traffic along the riverbanks. The wood yard man no longer able to sell his cords for cash on the nail, became a victim of progress.

In calculating the fuel, a measuring stick eight feet in length was used. Ten lengths equalled twenty cords if it was fairly piled. An acre of good woodland yielded one hundred cords of wood. According to a report published in a river paper, the fuel bill for one particular boat was two hundred dollars a week on the upper Ohio but only eighty dollars a week on the Mississippi because of riverside wood availability.

About two thirds of all steamboats throughout the steamboat era were owned by four men or less, and normally one fourth of the boats were owned by single proprietors. Operations, although limited to the rivers, were a practically and economically run. The steamboat businessman's main outlay was that of the boat alone. No right of way or terminal facilities were required. A new and fully equipped steamboat of average size would cost no more than a single mile of well built railroad track. The most practical boat was the packet, designed to carry both passengers and cargo, and normally operating a regular run at stated intervals. Steamboat operations were organized territorially into what were known as "trades." A trade was simply a field of operations between two ports. The im-

The packet *Chaperon*, ca. 1905.

Poster advertising the steamer, *Zanetta*.

A typical pictorial letterhead, this one of the
Streckfus Line in use in 1916.

portance of a trade depended less on the distance spanned, than on the volume of traffic carried. Packet operators also formed loose associations to run what became known as a "line service." Line arrangements were usually conceived during the periods of idleness when low water forced most boats to tie up, bringing steamboat owners and captains together at the larger ports. The boats forming the line were usually separately owned, but within the agreement, independently operated. The service consisted simply of two or more steamboats offering packet service on a given route or trade. It filled the need for a more frequent service than a lone packet could give, producing a more evenly distributed service than a number of packets operating separately. It was usually arranged to provide daily, thrice-weekly, or semi-weekly departures in each direction depending on the length of the trade. The line service was not the success which many hoped it would be due to constant squabbles over the variations in traffic. The participants were often unstable characters who would back out, or break up completely with little provocation. This situation was not helped by the action of the freelancers, known as "transients" or "tramps" who roved from trade to trade wherever business beckoned, without any field of operations, and without schedule or regularity. Transient operations appealed to the businessman of little means. With his capital invested in a vessel he could commence operations without delay, and with minimal preparation. He could assemble a skeleton crew, lay in supplies and tie up at a wharf to await cargo. He did not require any terminal facilities such as offices, freight sheds or passenger depots—he merely placed a poster announcing his destination and date of departure, possibly backed up by an advertisement in the local press. Quite often the boat served as his home as well as his place of business.

Steamboats did not escape the attentions of the reform movements. The effect was felt in the early 1840s and culminated in the introduction of "temperance boats." In these boats the customary bar was either eliminated or was converted to a soda fountain serving ice cream and non-alcoholic beverages. There were even boats crewed entirely by teetotallers.

Business methods to attract passengers were frequently unethical. Towns were placarded with colorful posters, and touts for competing lines made the levees active. Rival runners raced to secure passenger's baggage, hurrying it aboard. Sometimes the passengers found themselves on one boat and their luggage on another, and husbands and wives were often separated. Nervous old ladies, scared of boiler explosions, were told the boat had no boilers by conniving boatmen. Life on steamboats generally contrasted the exalted claims of the owners. One traveler on the *Gallant* referred to her as one of the filthiest of all rat-traps that he had ever traveled in. His companions were comprised of every type of backwoodsmen, gamblers and drunkards, with their ladies and babies of the same nature. They all washed in tin basins using the river water and only one cake of soap, drying themselves on the one solitary roller towel. The stateroom, he declared was better fitted for the smoking of hams. When it rained outside, it rained within and the passengers hurriedly sought a spot free from the many spouts overhead.

Frances Trollope in her *Domestic Manners of the Americans*, wrote disparagingly of her fellow passengers: "Let no one who wishes to receive agreeable impressions of American manners commence his travels in a Mississippi steamboat; for myself, it is with all sincerity I declare, that I would infinitely prefer sharing the apartment of well-conditioned pigs to the being confined to its cabin."

The earnings of steamboat captains were dependent upon freight rates which fluctuated constantly. These rates were governed in the main, by four factors; the amount of freight on hand, the number of steamboats in the trade, the stage of the water and the season of the year. The first two factors were subject to competition and the law of supply and demand. With a plentiful supply of freight on hand and a good stage of water, the regular boats would charge a rate sufficiently high to yield a handsome return. Thereupon transient, or wild boats as they were commonly called, would put in an appearance seeking to capture a share of the trade. So long as freight was plentiful and competition not a factor, the traffic remained normal, but when freight became scarce, either the regular or the wild boats would start cutting their rates. Cutthroat competition became the order of the day, and a season which might have started with a downstream tariff of twenty-five cents for a given weight would drop to five cents. While this price was ruinous to steamboat owners, the shippers who pocketed the savings rubbed their hands with joy. Passenger fares likewise fluctuated depending upon the number of passengers wishing to use the service. Downstream rates were usually about half the upstream rate. Both of these charges rose when the water levels dropped and cut as the levels rose.

It was not uncommon in the 1830s for boats to be attacked by Indians on the upper Mississippi. The Indians would lie hidden along the banks of the river, opening fire with guns as soon as the boat came within range, splattering the sides and upper works with bullets. In these situations the pilot was in great danger. If he made an error or lost his nerve his boat could end up on a sandbar or run into the bank and massacre. In such instances the true art of piloting was revealed.

Upstream cargoes on the upper Mississippi, included the personal possessions of the many immigrants making their way west. There were also steadily mounting shipments of manufactured goods from the east, along with European imports. Farm tools and machinery, animals and seed corn, barrels of nails, stoves, even complete sawmills were listed in the manifests, as well as rakes, hoes, spades, axes, grindstones, ox yokes, ploughs, and in later days, reapers and mowers. Livestock on board included oxen, so fat they could hardly walk, cows, calves, horses, mules, sheep, pigs, turkeys, geese, ducks, and hens, most of which were accommodated on the lower deck, adding to the deck passengers' misery. (Needless to say, the cabin passengers did not enjoy the disagreeable odors emanating from below either.) Delivery of unaccompanied freight away from the organized wharfs did present some problems. It became accepted practice simply to land cargo on the bare riverbank preferably out of reach of a sudden rise. A request to a local inhabitant to pass the word on to the consignee or a blast from the whistle relieved the captain of any further responsibility. Mail service never achieved a dominant position in the cargo of paddle steamers. The financial aid of mail contracts did not compensate for the regularity of service the mail contracts demanded. Repeated failures to observe the conditions of contract led to

the gradual withdrawal of mail routes from the rivers, and in any event the emergent railway system offered a more reliable service.

Paddle steamers were frequently used to move Indian tribes from territory taken over by the Westward migration of settlers. Steamboat captains reaped a harvest whenever whole tribes were transported on their boats, because of the guaranteed cargo and payment by the United States government. Supplies granted the tribes usually included barrels of flour, pork, salt, lard, kegs of tobacco, bales of blankets, guns and ammunition, axes and ploughs, corn, and cash, all of which was transported by the steamer.

With the end of the steamboat era, the river towns lost their personal touch with the river. The public landing points, once an ever changing panorama of people and merchandise on the move, lost their attraction as a social meeting place. The magnitude of this activity can be understood by the recorded traffic through Cincinnati in 1852: 8,000 arrivals were logged—about one every hour. To the general public, the paddle steamer was more than just a means of transport; by the standards of the day it was a marvelously fast and comfortable means of locomotion. When a steamboat announced its coming with a long blast of the whistle, there was something special about its arrival which was absent from the noisy appearance of a train. But with all their noteworthy qualities, the river paddle steamers had several major operational weaknesses: they burned fuel inefficiently, wore out quickly, and suffered very high accident rates. These defects were in part the result of ignorance, the price to be paid for operating in a hostile environment and by-products of the pioneering process where mechanical progress advanced beyond the limits of technical knowledge. Poor design, faulty construction and rough handling all contributed to the difficulties. The paddle steamer was an instrument which gave momentum to an advancing frontier, the building of towns, growth of trade and manufacturing industries, all of which would have taken place without it, but at a much slower pace, akin to the progress of the flatboat and keelboat, or the tedious advance of the stagecoach and waggontrain. The growth of the West and the rise in steamboat transportation were inseparable. Although towards the end, the railroad was the nat-

Lithograph by J. C. Wild, of Front Street, St. Louis, 1840, showing Market House and river trade. (Courtesy of Missouri Historical Society.)

A levee scene at Nashville, Tennessee. The steamers
left to right are the *J. B. Richardson*, the *Bob Dudley*
and the *H. W. Buttorf*. (Courtesy of S & D Reflector,
from the Captain Sam G. Smith collection.)

Poster advertising the *Grand Republic*. (From the
collection of the Public Library of Cincinnati and
Hamilton County.)

STEAMER
GRAND REPUBLIC
W. H. THORWEGEN, COMMANDER.
THE LARGEST STEAMBOAT IN THE WORLD.
WILL STORE 12000 BALES OF COTTON.

March 1st to August 1st. REGULAR PACKET between St. Louis and New Orleans, leaving St. Louis every third Saturday.

October 1st to March 1st. Regular MEMPHIS & NEW ORLEANS COTTON PACKET, leaving Memphis every alternate Wednesday, leaving New Orleans every alternate Friday.

HULL 350 FEET LONG.
FREIGHT CAPACITY 4000 TONS.

CABIN 300 FEET LONG.
30 FEET WIDE. 18 FEET HIGH.

ural enemy of the steamboats there were occasions when they co-operated for the common good. Such an occasion came to light when a steamboat sank in Ohio. The railroad laid on, in the middle of a January night, a special train to search the shore for survivors. On the other side of the coin, steamboats had been known to pick up railroad passengers who were stranded due to floods. With the loss of the bulk of the passenger trade to the railroads, the steamboat moved into the towing trade, transporting bulk cargoes over long distances. This in turn bred a new type of steamer, specially designed to push large tows fitted out with powerful engines. Some such boats built around the turn of the cen-

tury survived fifty years. One of the largest tows was the one made by the stern-wheeler *Joseph B. Williams*, in 1882. It comprised a mixture of coal boats, barges and fuel boats, 37 pieces in all, carrying 26,000 tons of coal. It had an overall length including the paddle steamer of 862 feet, and was 258 feet wide. Thirty years later the mammoth towboat *Sprague*, with a fleet of sixty coal boats and barges, 925 feet long and 312 feet wide, moved a cargo of 67,307 tons of coal. The area covered by this tow was nearly seven acres. After World War II, the diesel-powered towboat appeared. With its even greater horsepower and load capacity, it soon pushed the steam towboats into obscurity.

Towboat *A. R. Budd* with loaded coalboats towed "duckpond" style at Sewickey, Pennsylvania, ca. 1916. The mate at the front of the tow used voice and arm signals to assist the pilot in navigating the tow. (From the Collection of the Public Library of Cincinnati & Hamilton County.)

The steamboat *Sprague*, the largest towboat ever to ply the Mississippi River, and possibly the largest steam towboat in the world. Built at Dubuque, Iowa, in 1901, and completed at St. Louis in June, 1902, she was affectionately known among rivermen as "Big Momma." Her dimensions were 276 feet by 61 feet by 7.4 feet. She was fitted with two tandem compound engines developing two thousand indicated horse power. Her 36 feet diameter paddle wheel was said to weigh 160 tons. The forty-foot wide paddle wheel operated at eleven revolutions per minute. Taken out of service in 1948, she was later donated by the Standard Oil Company to Vicksburgh, Mississippi. She was then fitted out as a theatre and museum but suffered a disastrous fire in 1974. Then, after being refloated, she was beached. After being refloated again for restoration her hull cracked with the strain and she again sank. A sympathetic reporter, after visiting the wreck, wrote: "She is deteriorating more and more, the paddle wheel is off and in the water about 300 feet downstream. It's a dismal sight and the idea of restoration becomes more ludicrous with each passing day. It's looking more and more as though she will be scrapped on the spot." It is believed that any plans to rehabilitate the *Sprague* have been abandoned. (Photograph courtesy of S & D Reflector.)

A sad end for the mighty Sprague. The above photographs were taken in October, 1980 on the Yazoo River in Vicksburgh. (Photographs by Fred D. Fleming, courtesy of S & D Reflector.)

During the first twenty years of the paddle steamer era the amount of regularly scheduled operations was small. Long trips were made by individual boats on a one-off basis announced well in advance. Usually a departure date was given but very often the boat departed only when sufficient cargo had been accumulated to make the trip financially viable. This hit and miss arrangement led to some packet operators forming loose associations to run what became known as a line service. The boats forming the line were usually separately owned, but within the agreement independently operated, the owner being responsible for all running costs. Such a service consisted simply of two or more steamboats offering packet service on a given route or "trade." This arrangement permitted a more frequent and reliable service than a lone packet could give and it provided a more evenly distributed service than a number of packets operating separately.

Throughout the era, line operations in general lacked permanence; they were not the success that many had hoped and several broke up due to internal squabbles. Paddle steamer operations were beset with many difficulties, such as ice in the winter and low water states in the summer which caused boats to be laid up. Many of those laid up were destroyed at their moorings by ice gorges and the frailty of these boats was only too obvious when abnormal conditions prevailed resulting in many sinkings. The advance of the railroads which ran to a regular uninterrupted schedule was one of the major reasons for financial failure. Competition by the latter only served to increase competition within the steamboat business, and although in exceptional circumstances a boat could cover the cost of its construction in one trip, line operations sometimes could not even reach the break even figure. Was it any wonder that with this background the high hopes and good intentions of newly formed lines often foundered before the end of their first season? Mergers, liquidations and break ups were legion. Indeed if one looks into the history of some lines it is difficult to trace a common thread, as mergers were more often entered into for mutual survival than planned expansion. In retrospect out of this minefield of obstacles it was a miracle that any of the lines survived for any length of time. The formation of the line operations brought many advantages to both operators and their clients. The operator benefitted from the slightly higher rates and fares obtained by running his boats on a regular schedule, and secondly from the connections and goodwill which such a stable business provided. Line service simplified operating problems and enabled the crew to enjoy a more settled mode of living. It was also popular with the business community who could move their services and wares on schedule, and last it attracted trade to the commercial centers from which the boats operated.

Different boats in sequence often carried the same name. Boats changed ownership in liquidations and mergers, and over a period of time it would appear that company names were either duplicated or abbreviated. The confusion thus caused makes research of the line operations a trap for the unwary. Thus, the following outlines of companies engaged in the steamboat business should be read as a general picture and not as an authoritative history.

The most notable line to prosper on the Ohio before the Civil War was the Pittsburgh and Cincinnati Packet Line formed in 1842. This line had its origin in the heavy westward immigrant traffic, originally composed of seven of the largest, fastest and finest steamboats on the upper Ohio. It continued in operation for over ten years, maintaining a daily departure in both directions, its schedule interrupted only by unfavorable river conditions. This fact was not overlooked by a Pittsburgh newspaper editor who complimented the line on its first five years of service by describing it as "the greatest convenience ever afforded the citizens on the banks of the upper Ohio." An advertisement for the line at this time boasted that it had carried a million persons without the least injury. The line reached its zenith in the early fifties when it ran such boats as the *Buckeye State* and the *Keystone State*. The year 1854 saw the start of railroad competition that made serious inroads into the companies operations on the Ohio. By 1855 most of the line's boats had departed for the more lucrative trade on the waters of the Mississippi. Even at this late stage efforts were made to merge with another steamboat company with the intention of extending the field of operations to St. Louis. Disagreements however led to the abandonment of this idea and by 1856 the line had been dissolved along with its intended partner.

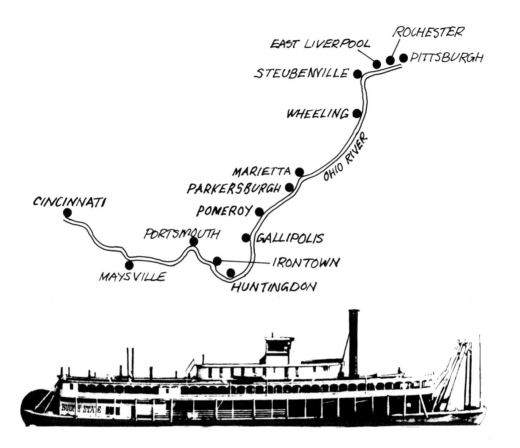

Pittsburgh and Cincinnati packet lines.
Ohio River trade.

Advertising poster listing boats and schedules of the
Pittsburgh & Cincinnati Packet Line. An unusual
feature of the poster was the illustrated boat, it is a
side-wheeler whereas the four boats listed were all
stern-wheelers. (Courtesy of S & D Reflector.)

The Eagle Packet Company, founded by two brothers, Henry and William Leyhe of Warsaw, Illinois, commenced operations on the Mississippi in 1861 with one boat, a stern-wheeler named the *Young Eagle*. It operated on the short five-mile run from Warsaw to Keokuk, Iowa. In 1865 they expanded their operations with the purchase of a new boat, the *Grey Eagle*, which ran daily between Canton, Missouri and Quincy, Illinois. By 1873 their business was so successful that they had a new side-wheeler built at Madison, Indiana, at a cost of thirty thousand dollars. Named the *Spread Eagle* it was placed in the St. Louis, Alton, and Grafton daily trade and the company offices moved to Alton, Illinois. A report appearing in the *Daily Gate City* newspaper, in Keokuk on May 23, 1875, read as follows. "The reconstructed *Eagle*, of the Eagle Line, will arrive on her first trip tomorrow evening. It is reported that she is now the fastest boat on the river." The *Quincy Herald* says of her: "Capt. Henry Leyhe's *Eagle* arrived from St. Louis yesterday, and is certainly one of the handsomest little crafts ever seen on these waters. [She] is the largest of the Eagle Company's boats and will take the place of the steamer *De Smet*, in the Quincy and Keokuk trade. The boat has been furnished with new and powerful machinery, and is not only one of the handsomest but fastest boats on the river. She has been handsomely painted, and has all the appearance of a new boat. Her cabin is conveniently arranged with a number of state rooms along each side. A handsome set of furniture has been selected for the ladies cabin, so this boat can compare very favorably with any boat on the Mississippi."

During subsequent years this successful line not only added several new boats to their fleet but absorbed some of their competitors. In 1891 the line purchased the St. Louis, Naples & Peoria Packet Company, which operated on the Illinois River. Included in the sale was a wharfboat located at St. Louis, which became the Eagle Packet Line's base of operations. The next acquisition by the Leyhe brothers was the St. Louis & Mississippi Packet Company in 1894, thus expanding the line downriver into the Cape Girardeau and Commerce trades. During 1903 a bad flood brought in extra business when the Alton Railroad with sections of their track under water, chartered two boats, the *Bald Eagle* and the *Spread Eagle* to convey all passengers, perishables, milk and mail between Alton and St. Louis until the flood water receded. The 1904 St. Louis World's Fair boosted the company's passenger business when the daily run of the *Spread Eagle* to Grafton became a popular excursion for the visitors. When the automobile and the truck running on paved roads added further competition the packet trade declined drastically.

Formed in 1858, the St. Louis & St. Joseph Union Packet Line was composed of twelve Missouri River steamboats: the *A. B. Chambers, Dan Lewis, D. A. January, Hesperian, Kate Howard, Minnehaha, Morning Star, Peerless, Silver Heels, Southwestern, Sovereign* and *Twilight*. Their primary trade was a long one between St. Louis and St. Joseph, a river distance of 498 miles. The Missouri River was one of the most difficult and dangerous of all the Mississippi valley rivers to navigate. It was plagued with snags, sand bars, caving banks, and rapid currents, with the added hazard of negotiating the newly built railroad bridges. These risks were balanced against the need for transportation demanded by the emigrants moving west, inducing many owners to form the line service, it also attracted boats from beyond the trade. The St. Louis & St. Joseph Union Packet Line did however, build up a reputation for its class of boat and regular service. Such a regularly maintained service was unique on this river. Nevertheless, in time the shortcomings of the line became apparent; the limited navigable season, plus the many hazards combined with the long distances involved, soon caused consternation as to the practicality of trying to sustain the line. Boats could be withdrawn from the service at the option of the owners and cooperation within the line deteriorated. In the circumstances the break up was a foregone conclusion.

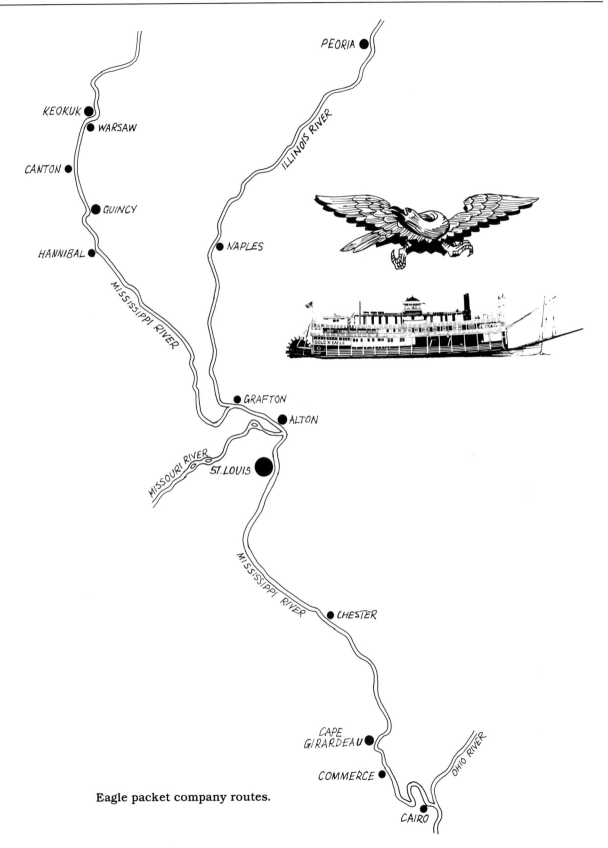

Eagle packet company routes.

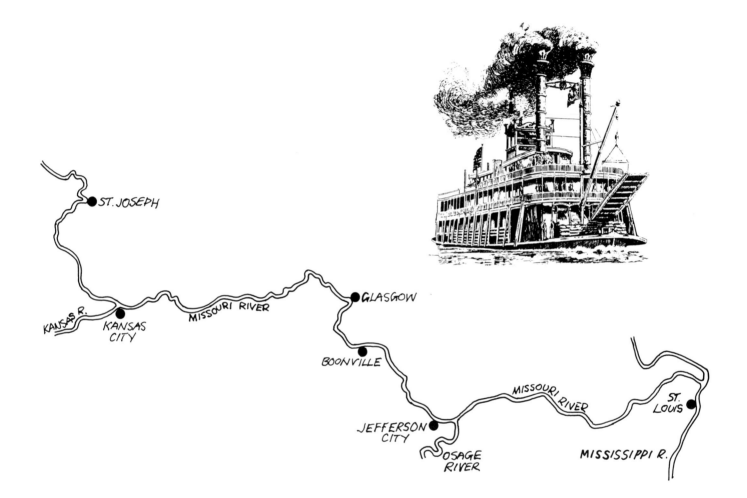

The Missouri trades,
St. Louis and St. Joseph Union Packet Line.

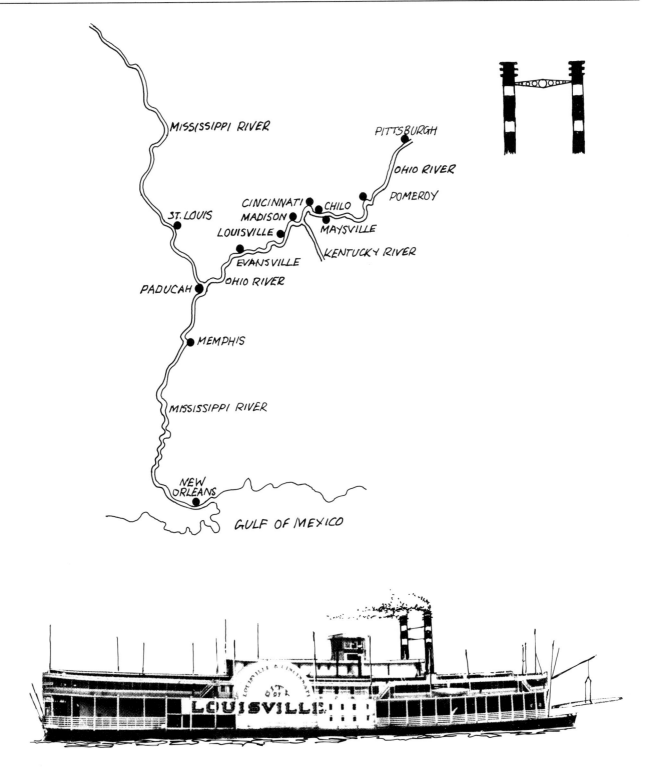

**The Cincinnati, Portsmouth, Big Sandy
and Pomeroy Packet Company.**

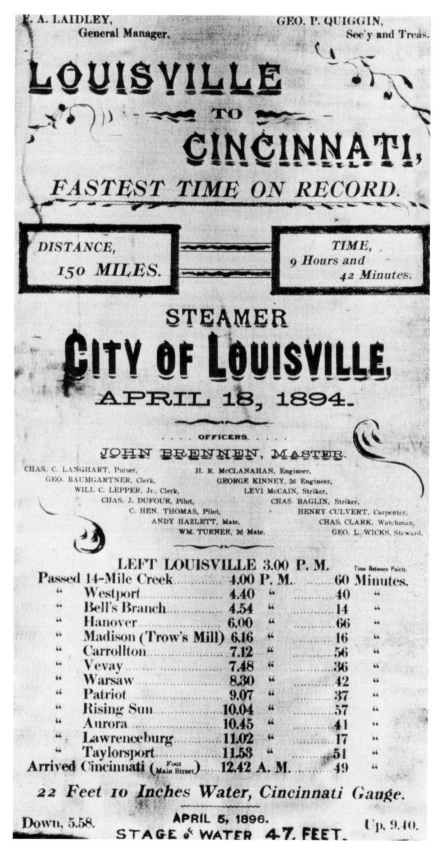

An original of this memorial display hung in the cabin of the *City of Louisville.* It recorded her record-breaking trip. (Courtesy of S. & D Reflector.)

The Cincinnati, Portsmouth, Big Sandy & Pomeroy Packet Company, a rather unwieldy name which outlined the early route traveled by the first of the company's boats, was commonly referred to throughout the river valleys as the White Collar Line, and at a later date it became the Louisville & Cincinnati Packet Co. In 1889 the White Collar Line ran twenty-two steamboats all marked by the identifying pair of white bands, or collars, around the tops of their smokestacks. With Cincinnati as their home port, White Collar Line steamers ran to Pittsburgh, Charleston, Louisville, Evansville, and Paducha on the Ohio, and from St. Louis to New Orleans on the Mississippi. It was the day of magnificent, passenger-carrying steamers, fare wars with competing lines, and hotly-run races with rival packets. At a later stage the Cincinnati, Portsmouth, Big Sandy, & Pomeroy Packet Company gained control of the Louisville & Cincinnati Packet Company, formerly known as the U.S. Mail Line, whose boats operated in the profitable trade between Cincinnati and Louisville. In 1894 the company purchased a new boat, a magnificent side-wheeler which they named the *City of Louisville*. She was 300 feet long, and boasted 72 staterooms with a capacity of 160 passengers. She set the all-time speed records between Cincinnati and Louisville in both directions. Her sister ship, the *City of Cincinnati* which maintained the same high standard, was built in 1899. These two boats became famous for the excellence of their cuisine, and it was not unusual to have 200 or more diners for the evening meal. The arrival and departure of these glamorous steamers attracted crowds to the riverfront. Another boat, the *Indiana* joined the fleet in 1900. Slightly smaller than the other two (only 285 feet long), she served as the low water boat in the trade.

Many factors contributed to the success of the White Collar Line, not least of which was the quality of the service rendered. All of the boats were dependable, well kept, and efficiently managed and were great favorites with the traveling public. Also a profitable venture was the Sunday excursion, made attractive by a round trip fare of fifty cents, with good meals at the same price. Boats in the Cincinnati and Louisville trade carried cargo in small quantities, quicker and for less money than the competing railroads.

The packets also had good connections with the packets of other lines, as well as local railroads, which enabled them to ship freight to points beyond their territory. In addition to the three principal boats running in the Louisville trade the White Collar Line had the side-wheelers *Bonanza*, *Bostona*, and *Telegraph*, and the stern-wheelers *Sunshine* and *Sherley* running to Pomeroy; the impressive *New South*, a side-wheeler to Memphis; the *Henry M. Stanley* to Charleston; the *Courier* to Maysville, Kentucky; the *Lizzie Bay* to Madison, Indiana; the *Tacoma* to Chilo, Ohio and the *Dick Brown* to the Kentucky River. Other large stern-wheel packets made the longer trips to Pittsburgh and New Orleans. By 1904 the intensive competition from rival lines and railroads success in creaming off both passenger and freight business caused the company to sell the trades above Cincinnati to the Greene Line. The two leading boats, the *City of Louisville* and the *City of Cincinnati* were wrecked when they were crushed in a massive ice jam that hit the Cincinnati riverfront in January 1918. The *Indiana* burned at the foot of Main Street in Cincinnati in May, 1916.

One of the most successful of the pre-Civil War lines was the St. Louis & New Orleans Packet Company, established in 1858. The line comprised ten of the finest steamers on the waters, which were all separately owned but "run in a joint interest," possibly under a central management with an arrangement for pooling receipts. The line at this time ran the following boats: the *A. T. Lacy*, the *Alex Scott*, the *City of Memphis*, the *Imperial*, the *J. C. Swan*, the *New Falls City*, the *New Uncle Sam*, the *Pennsylvania*, the *W. M. Morrison*, and the *James E. Woodruff*. The *Woodruff* had the unique distinction of being the first steamboat to publish a daily paper on board. This company earned the nickname, the "Railroad Line" because of its contracts with the Ohio & Mississippi Railroad at St. Louis and the Illinois Central at Cairo by which passengers and freight were contracted to all points reached by boat or railroad. Many forebodings were expressed as to its success, it being the first line to explore this cooperative venture. It was well managed, however, and in a very short time the arrangement became popular with both passengers and shippers everywhere. It ran on schedule with a regularity hitherto unknown in

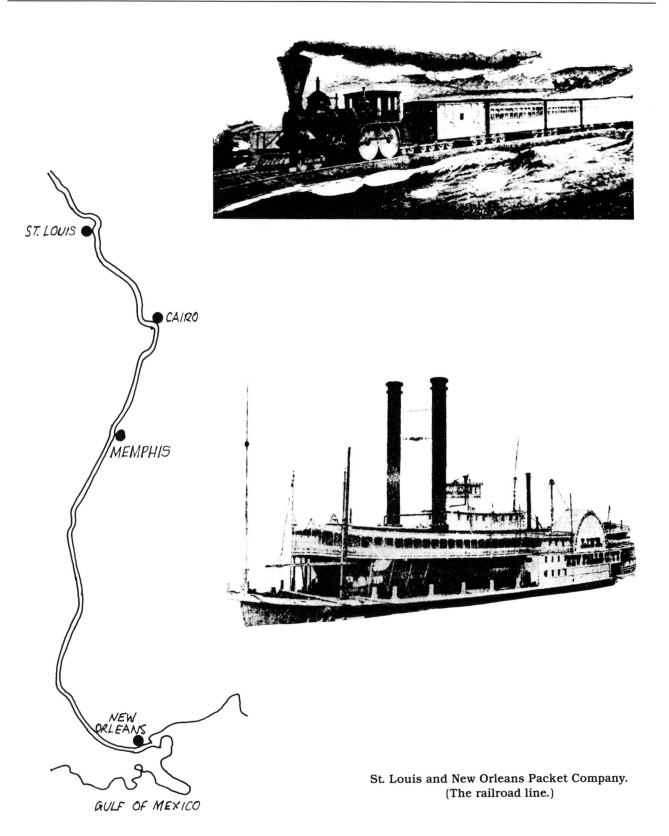

ST. LOUIS

CAIRO

MEMPHIS

NEW
ORLEANS

GULF OF MEXICO

St. Louis and New Orleans Packet Company.
(The railroad line.)

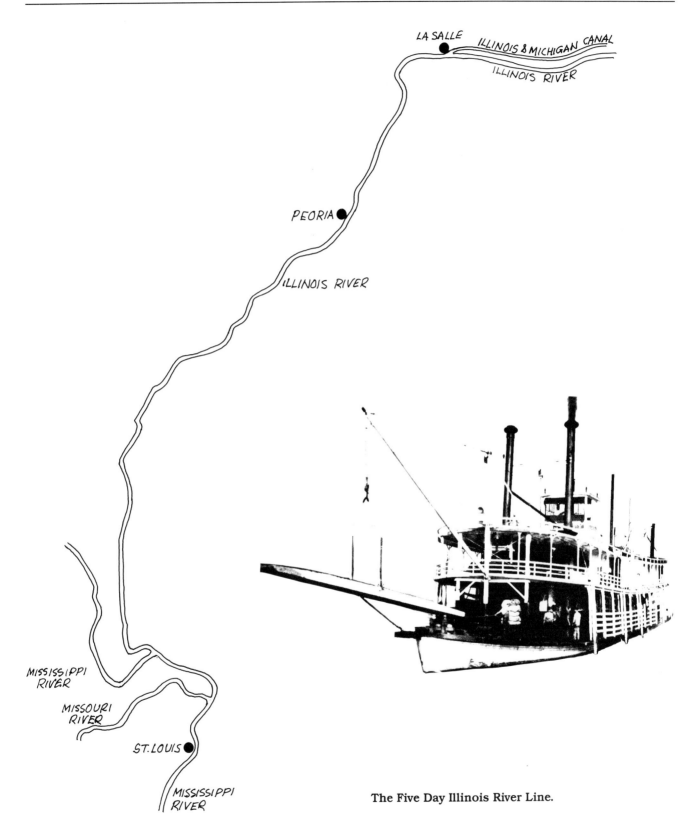

The Five Day Illinois River Line.

this trade, and at uniform rates. The line operated at a profit, until the outbreak of the Civil War caused its demise.

In 1852 what was known as the Five Day Line was organized to run the trade between St. Louis and La Salle, the head of navigation on the Illinois River. La Salle was also the terminus of the Illinois & Michigan Canal. An important link in east–west travel, this connection was rendered necessary to accommodate the move west. Patronage of the five-day line continued to increase, until railroad facilities were able to provide a more direct and faster route. The line was owned by individual companies, each boat being separately accountable. Some of the finest and fastest boats served this trade and the time made by some of them from St. Louis to La Salle has never been equalled on the Illinois River. The title, the Five Day Line originated in the fact that prior to its establishment the trip took a whole week. Therefore, to reduce the time to five days was a great improvement, and it was not accepted by the members without some apprehension. It was only through great persuasion that the change was made and then only under protest by the older members. It was in the spirit of the age and the arrangement became normal routine. A few years of intensive railroad competition finally destroyed the famous line along with others on the Illinois River.

7

A long with the benefits of faster and more comfortable travel by steamboat, came the inevitable, but unforeseen accidents. River accidents during 1811–1851 fell into four main categories: collision—4.5%; fire—17%; explosion—21%; snags and other obstructions—57.5%. The worst period for steamboat casualties was from 1830–1839 when 272 were destroyed after less than three years of travel. Collisions were often brought about by the need for a boat to pick the deepest or fastest channel in the shallow rivers. Much confusion was caused by the lack of a uniform code of signaling, and signals were often misinterpreted by the pilot. Occasional poor visibility was also a contributing factor. Boats going in opposite directions reacted differently to currents and quite often crossed bows trying to follow their intended courses. A rising river is higher in the center than at the sides causing boats to drift toward the banks. When the river is falling the opposite is true. Collisions caused more damage to the vessels than to passengers and crew. Any loss of life was usually a result of people falling off the boat. There were no lifeboats or belts, and few people could swim. Steamboat captains were frequently upbraided by the press for failing to turn back when a passenger fell overboard. Captains seldom turned back at the cry of "man overboard," not out of mere indifference, but because of the general consensus that the paddle wheel rarely missed its mark. Isolated instances of survival after falling overboard were reported but they were very rare.

Fires were an ever present hazard on steamboats. All the ingredients to feed a blaze were there: a wooden boat with a flimsy, flammable superstructure, covered with coat upon coat of paint, and carrying a cargo of cotton, hay or spirits, and piles of wood. The boilers were at the center of the flashpoint, it only needed a hot ember to shoot out from the stokehold, or a spark from the high chimney to fall unobserved into the right place to set off an inferno. The hemp tiller ropes presented a further hazard. Once alight they spread the fire forward to the pilot house or aft to the engine room. Even more disastrous, when the ropes burned through, the pilot would be unable to steer for the bank. In 1841 the *Rochester* had its wheel ropes replaced by chains, the first to be installed aboard a steamboat. This safety precaution set a precedent for other boats.

Moored craft were subject to additional hazards in the crowded levees where boats were tied up with little or no space between them. If one boat caught fire it would quickly ignite the other steamers. The largest such disaster occurred at St. Louis in 1849. It was a night of terror; an event referred to ever afterward as "The Great Fire." It began at about ten o'clock on the evening of May 17, and burned out of control throughout the night into early morning. The onshore fire first struck the steamer *White Cloud*. In a very short time the *Eudora*, moored astern, was ablaze. The *Edward Bates* then caught fire. Someone may have cut the *Bates* adrift in the hope of saving the other boats, or perhaps her hawsers burned. Nevertheless, a strong wind quickly blew her back to shore and like a flaming torch she set light to all of the boats moored to the levee. By the time the holocaust was over, twenty-three boats and several onshore buildings were laid

to waste. As a result of the fire, the city of St. Louis passed an ordinance compelling all boats to use iron hawsers when tying up.

The most spectacular steamboat disasters were caused by exploding boilers. The suddenness, and immense force would attract the morbid curiosity of the public. Flying wreckage, scalding water, escaping steam and cries from the injured added to the excitement. This indeed was good copy for the press, more so since up to three hundred lives could be lost in a major explosion. Excessive pressure, lack of water in the boilers, safety valve failures, and general lack of scientific understanding of the problems in this new form of power, were the basic reasons for such catastrophies. In the early days the boiler water level was ascertained by the use of the gauge stick, a broom handle. There were three gauges situated in the end of the boiler. They were about three inches apart vertically, the lowest one just above the water line. When the gauge stick was pushed against them a valve would open allowing steam and water to escape into a short tin trough underneath. The boiler would then be topped up according to the readings. Steam gauges did not come into general use until 1852, when the Steamboat Inspection Act came into force.

Sometimes disasters occurred which owed nothing to the ignorance of man, and everything to the caprice of nature. Accidents caused by snags fell into this category. Snags are formed when the erosive action of the current undermine the banks, causing whole trees to fall into the river. In the turbulent environment of a flooded river, these trees lose their limbs and branches, and their buoyancy. The heavy gravel-enmeshed roots sink to the bottom and form snags, the top of the tree often honed to a point by the abrasive action of the silt. Driftwood became a tremendous problem in the flood seasons. It was carried into the deepest and swiftest parts of the river where it was most difficult to avoid. Apart from damage to hulls, driftwood was a major cause of paddle wheel damage also, but fortunately was not responsible for any loss of life. Snags could cause minor damage to paddle wheels and guards, but the worst damage occurred when they penetrated the hull. Some of these dangerous snags were as large as tree trunks, and as much as seventy-five feet long, waterlogged and extremely heavy. These jagged spears with the heavy end embedded on the bottom, lay poised and ready to rip open the hull and sink the luckless vessels. An example of the danger from such snags is best illustrated by the story of the *Banner State*. In 1852, (as reported in the *Louisville Courier*) on its way up river from New Orleans, it struck a snag which "went up through the starboard guard, turned eight passengers out of their beds, at the same time bursting the staterooms to splinters, continuing its course upward through the hurricane roof, cut the texas in two, and disappeared over the other side of the boat." Miraculously none of the passengers aboard *Banner State* was hurt. This type of snag could usually be seen during daylight hours; thus the most dangerous time was at night. If a breached hull could not be quickly repaired with a temporary bulkhead, the only way to save the boat from going to the bottom was to close up the hole with blankets or mattresses.

The flotsam brought down the rivers by the floods added further dangers to the paddle steamers. In addition to the expected uprooted trees, farms and houses were often gulped by the hungry river. Cabins half submerged, furniture, fences, chicken coops and rafts, dead and half alive animals, and occasionally human bodies added to the horrible parade.

In the 1840s, the arrival of an adapted diving bell enabled salvage of sunken vessels that previously had been written off. Initially, the apparatus was used to recover cargo, but within a decade, with the addition of powerful pumps, vessels could be raised, refloated, and returned to service. The diving bell was rapidly superseded by the invention of the armored diving suit and helmet with glass windows. This enabled a diver to go below and carry out repairs prior to pumping out and raising the vessel. From those small beginnings special salvage steamboats were developed. One such boat, the *T. F. Eckert* owned by the Cincinnati underwriters, raised and removed 360 wrecked steamboats, barges and other vessels over a ten year period, recovering some 20,000 tons of machinery and cargo. The repair problems were aggravated by the long distances covered in the principal trades, and by the thinly populated country through which steamboats passed on trips that often lasted several weeks. Not only were towns of any importance few in number, in most instances their repair fa-

cilities were limited to simple blacksmith equipment and were of little value in major repairs, such as a broken shaft, crank or piston. If the hull were still afloat after any of the aforementioned disasters, providing it could be towed to a boatyard, it would be pulled up on the bank broadside, placed on a series of cradles, and mounted on rails. The whole assembly would then be winched out of the water, the hull inspected, and repairs made. These "marine ways" were usually permanent installations in the larger towns, so the location of the wreck in the early days had a bearing on its survival. Floating dry docks were introduced at a few locations in the 1830s but little is known about their popularity. A stationary dry dock was built in connection with the canal at Louisville.

Old boat wrecks also added to the dangers on the rivers. A report from around 1875 stated that on stretch of the Mississippi between St. Louis and Cairo, wrecks averaged one a mile over hundreds of miles.

"Sawyers," trees embedded into the river with projecting branches, were particularly dangerous obstructions. They were the result of erosive action undermining the trees along the river bank, causing them to slip into the water. These could be more deadly than other snags, due to the greater speed of the downstream-bound steamboats. Captain Henry M. Shreve, to whom most historians

Captain Henry M. Shreve, designer of the first steam powered snagboat and supervisor in the removal of the Red River raft.

credit the beginning of the steamboat era because of his development of the first successful light draught riverboat, was also responsible for the design and construction of a snagboat. This was specially designed to remove the snags and sawyers from the rivers. Given the name *Heliopolis* it started working about 1829. The *Heliopolis* had twin hulls placed side by side. The bows were connected at the water line by a heavy wedge-shape snagbeam which was the chief weapon against the deeply embedded snags of the Mississippi. Another snagboat, the *Archimedes* built by Shreve was designed for use in low water having a more shallow draught than the *Heliopolis*. When going into action, the snagboat would run full speed at the projecting snag, catching it on the snagbeam and forcing it out of the water. The snag was then lifted by a powerful winch and cut up. Snags weighing as much as seventy tons were easily disposed of by these boats which became known as "Uncle Sam's Toothpullers." The *Archimedes* proved a great success, and with this boat Shreve quickly cleared the Ohio and then the Mississippi. Since these obstructions accounted for more wrecks than any other cause, his action was a major factor in the increase of river trading. In the early 1830s Captain Shreve reported that some snags in the river weighed as much as one hundred tons. In 1833 he gathered together a group of steamboats, flatboats and keelboats and set out to break up the Red River "Raft"—a major obstruction on the Red River, beginning at boggy Bayou and extending 165 miles upstream to the Carolina Buffs. The Red River rose in western Texas, cut across the lower corner of Arkansas then turned south into Louisiana. In the middle of Louisiana it spread into a vast swamp and a series of stagnant bayous covering about two hundred miles. The swampland was created by a great raft, a solid platform of tangled trees in the river's channel which had started to form centuries before. It was said to be so solid in places that horsemen could cross without being aware that they were crossing a river. Although he cleared the first seventy miles in a few months, it was not until the spring of 1838 that the work was completed, and the Red River Raft cleared out.

Rivermen lived in fear lest steamboats, wharfboats and ferries be destroyed by innumerable ice gorges formed when the ice broke up. The impact of tons of floating ice frequently crushed and sank steamboats at their moorings, or swept them downstream. Ideally steamboats sought the shelter of lagoons, swamps or small tributaries off the major river before the big freeze got under way. A watchman was often left on guard accompanied by a small group of workmen who made the necessary repairs to the boat in readiness for the next season. During the winter of 1917–1918 the Ohio valley experienced the worst winter in fifty years. The river was heavily frozen, and in the ice jam that followed at Cincinnati a great number of woodenhulled steamboats, including the *City of Cincinnati* and *City of Louisville* were crushed and lost in the ice. It was later recorded that within the Cincinnati Engineers District, 191 wrecks occurred as a result of the ice. A report published in a Memphis newspaper in 1872 read, "Calamity roared into Memphis harbour about one o'clock on the morning of December 27th. Jagged hunks of ice smashed and ground against each other, piled as much as ten feet above the water level; this mass of destruction was swept against the Memphis bank, wiping out every boat and barge on the water front."

Of all the obstructions to navigation sandbars were the most common. They were found in varying number and size throughout the river system, but normally in the lower part of rivers. Usually they formed at the head and foot of each island, at the mouth of large streams, and at many other places where the slowing down of the current caused the water to deposit some of its burden of sand and silt. Gravelbars, normally hard and permanent could also be loose and shifting, but were nevertheless more stable than sand bars although they formed a more formidable barrier. Rockbars occurred where rock strata extended into or across the river bed. Steamboats which ran afoul of these rarely escaped serious damage and often sank as a result. With the river in its normal state, most bars were well under the water and caused few problems. Even when the water level dropped, although presenting the steamboat with a problem, the bars could assist navigation by serving as dams. The dams effectively divided the river into a series of pools often many miles in length providing navigable water to sufficient depth for the paddle steamers to operate. In an effort to deepen the channel over a sandbar, experimental wing dams were constructed. These were made of timber and stone concentrating the flow of water at a low stage within a limited space without increasing the "expanse" of water and draining the pool above. The experiments proved successful, and many wing dams were constructed, resulting not only in easier navigation of the rivers, but in an increase of the depth of water, enabling additional tons of cargo to be carried.

The art of low-water navigation consisted largely in devising ways of getting the steamboat over bars. A tow line from a passing steamboat could be expensive and was usually avoided. The alternative was to use the capstan, pulling on a rope firmly secured on shore. Large trees were few and far between on the banks of the upper Missouri and in consequence an alternative anchoring point on which to warp the vessel had to be found. The boats carried heavy timber, to the center of which a cable known as the "dead man" was attached. It was taken forward to a point on the bank and buried. The capstan was then hauled in on the cable dragging the vessel over the obstruction. Before the introduction of the steam-driven capstan, a line was wrapped around the paddle wheel shaft allowing the power of the engine to be applied to the task. Grounding on sandbars was more of a problem than a disaster, but the difficulty led to some ingenious solutions. One method of freeing a grounded boat was known as "grasshoppering" or "walking the boat," using walking spars. Walking spars were of straight grained flawless yellow pine,

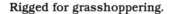

Rigged for grasshoppering.

The bow of a paddle steamer rigged for "grasshoppering." A spar chained or lashed to rings on the hull had a block mounted at its top and was hauled on by means of the capstan. When the head of the boat was raised an inch or so the boats' main engines were run to get her either over or back from the bar. Steamboats were usually loaded heavy at the head so that once the head cleared the bar the rest of the hull would pass over it.

shod with heavy iron points about a foot in length. They would grip the solid clay or gravel underlying the superficial layers of sand forming the bar. Where there was no bottom to the sand, an eighteen-inch diameter block would be used as a foot on the spar. A rope attached to the foot hauled the block up out of the sand after removal of the spar. The stout spar was placed over the bow, leaning in toward the boat. On the top end a pulley block was secured, and a long hawser joined it to another block secured to the foredeck. The crew then pulled on the hawser by use of the capstan lifting the bow off the sandbar. With the engines going ahead or astern the boat would be eased off or over the bar. A further improvement of this method involved two spars, one on either side. This way the bow was hauled up as before, but with the paddles churning at the stern to push the boat forward. At the same time, the churning paddles loosened the gravel and sand from under the hull drawing it back to clear a channel. In most cases the boat's advance was slow, and then the whole process had to be repeated again and again. Because boats were loaded heavier at the head, once the head was over the bar the rest of the boat would clear.

Low water navigation was a prolonged and tedious business, hard on all concerned. A traveler in the early 1930s reported that forty-seven hours instead of the usual eighteen were required to complete the one hundred thirty-five mile trip from Louisville to Cincinnati. On this trip the boat ran aground eleven times, lost both chimneys from striking tree branches along the shore, lost a crew member, injured another and met with a number of minor mishaps. The small amount of water necessary for the operation of light-draught steamboats was a source of no little humor. The purported ability of such vessels to run on a heavy dew became part of the steamboat traditions. When in 1859 a steamboat built for the Green River in Kentucky was shown to be capable of carrying ten tons of freight in just eight inches of water, her amused owners mounted a large watering can on the jackstaff to indicate the ease with which she could supply her own water when the river ran dry. The Missouri River is 2,945 miles in length, the longest river in North America. Conditions created by its geographical location earned it the doubtful honor of being the muddiest of all the rivers. Snow run-

ning off the high mountain areas around its head gave it two seasonal peaks one in April and another in June. For most of its course the river flows through windy, arid plains of alluvial soil with few trees or shrubs to stabilize the soil. In its upper reaches it is steep and fast flowing, but the long stretches in the Dakotas are relatively flat, shallow and meandering. The resultant suspended silt played havoc with the paddle steamers' boilers necessitating frequent stops to clear the accumulations or court disaster with falling steam pressure. The river was also afflicted with an unpredictable build up of sandbars. Grasshoppering was regularly practiced on the muddy Missouri.

Rapids presented formidable obstructions. They were at their worst in the very short season when the water was very high. If it had sufficient power the steamboat could get over with safety, providing the vessel had a pilot experienced in such conditions. Prior to cutting canals and locks to by-pass rapids, cargoes were unloaded then transferred to other vessels above and below the obstructions. At such points towns formed to provide this service. Provision of canals and locks eliminated one problem but created others. The size of a lock limited the size of paddle steamers, and in busy seasons long delays occurred amounting to days, and adding to the cost of operations.

Isolated rocks and boulders were minor hazards to navigation, provided their locations were known. The more dangerous of these were removed by blasting. Disastrous boiler explosions caused the greatest fear of steamboats, and inspired W. C. Redfield of Connecticut to devise the safety barge. This was built along the lines of the steamboat, but without power, and was towed by a steamboat. A company promoting this venture announced "Passengers on board the safety barges will not be in the least exposed to any accident by reason of the fire or steam on board the steamboats. The noise of the machinery, the trembling of the boat, the heat from the furnace, boilers and kitchen and everything which may be considered unpleasant on board a steamboat are entirely avoided." Progress by this mode of travel was slow. Unencumbered steamboats landed their passengers several hours before the safety barges. The novelty soon wore off, in spite of the improved safety, and the barges were converted to cargo carriers. Another attempt at removing the hazard of exploding boilers was to place the boilers on the guards, a practice that was used for many years. The advertisement for a boat in the *New Philadelphia* read, "She has a low pressure engine and her boilers are not on the boat, but are so placed over the water, on her guards which project from her sides, as to render it almost impossible that any passengers should receive injury from an accident to the boiler."

Steamboats were rarely wrecked by storms, but could be blown ashore suffering minor damage to the guards and upper workings. The shock of stopping abruptly, combined with a high wind often brought down chimneys. When a storm was approaching, the careful pilot acted quickly and sought protection on the sheltered shore. The vessel was moored to trees whereupon it rode out the storm, usually in safety. It was very rare for a boat to cap-

size, although there were frequent occasions when the pilot houses would be blown overboard, the luckless pilots with them. Stern-wheelers were especially difficult to handle in high winds, therefore a cautious pilot would remain in port until the storm abated. Fog could be a hazard to navigation depending on the character of the river. Pilots would have a choice of laying up at shore or, dependent on the force of the current, drifting until the fog cleared. Tornadoes were not unknown on the Mississippi and when they did occur paddle steamers had little or no defense, often being lifted bodily from the water, and dashed against the shore. Steamboats operating on the Missouri were often troubled by the abundant river silt that clogged the boiler valves and pipes. This condition resulted in many sinkings when propulsion was lost and the craft went out of control. Many steamboats were

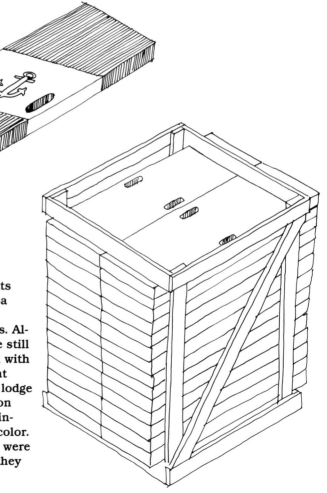

Every steamer carried life floats; excursion boats had hundreds of them. These were pine or balsa boards, one foot wide, three feet long, and two inches thick with hand holes cut into the edges. Although outlawed as new equipment, many were still in use through the 1960s. They were decorated with the boat's name and often were striped in bright colors. Silhouettes of animals, fouled anchors, lodge emblems and the like were frequently painted on them. They were hung on bulkheads ready for instant use where they made showy splashes of color. On passenger steamers, the great bulk of them were stored in racks. They were stacked loosely so they could float free in the event of a sinking.

Stern-wheeler *Virginia* stranded in a cornfield below Willow Grove, West Virginia, March 1910. The Ohio River was at a flood stage when the Virginia made a night time call at Willow Grove to off load a passenger and some cargo. She then cast off and while backing away the current turned her broadside and put her aground. Attempts to refloat her by unloading cargo plus the assistance of the towboat *Volcano* failed. The next day with the level falling she was firmly in ground. Six months later an attempt to get her back into the river by a specialist firm of house movers also ended in failure. The rains came shortly afterwards, the level of the Ohio rose, she floated and they steamed her back to Pittsburgh. (From the collection of the Public Library of Cincinnati and Hamilton County.)

struck by lightning but few caught fire. It was assumed that the charge on striking the stacks was earthed through iron boilers and machinery, then through the paddle wheel axle and into the river.

Some unusual paddle wheel accidents occurred that have become legendary. One such mishap took place aboard the *Flora* en route from Louisville to Wheeling on November 17, 1836, when the boiler supports gave way leaving the heavy boilers hanging by the steam connecting pipes. These broke and the escaping steam filled the social hall and cabins above. Two passengers died in this accident. When the one hundred and seventeen foot packed steamer *Neva* burned at Buffalo in 1908, her whistle continued to blow as she was consumed by flames. It was thought that a timber had fallen on the whistle valve causing her to sound her own death knell. A boat named the *Helen E* had a long runaway trip adrift on the January ice down the Ohio River without serious harm. The little packet was resting atop a large heavy ice floe and was thus protected on all sides.

To offset some of the danger lifeboats were fitted on a few riverboats as original equipment, but they were soon discarded as too big and awkward for river use. A simple skiff was better on every count. One could launch a dozen light rowboats in the time it took to read the instructions for operating a lifeboat davit. Doors and window shutters were usually hung on gravity hinges allowing rapid removal in an emergency. Many lives were saved by persons paddling to the shore on flotsam of this nature.

One of the worst nighttime collisions was between the steamers *Monmouth* and the *Warren* in 1837. It occurred in a bend on the lower Mississippi. The collision happened during a severe rainstorm. The *Monmouths* cabin broke in two as she was sinking, she had been engaged in the removal of the 'Creek Tribe' to the west from their former southern homeland. Of the 611 Indians aboard 300 were drowned.

The Missouri was always difficult to navigate, the bed of the river shifted constantly throughout its 2,600 miles length. During the fifty years of active steamboating nearly 500 vessels were lost between St. Louis and Fort Benton. Boats operating on this river could suffer frequent delays caused by herds of buffalo; thousands of the beasts forded the river.

In the early days of steamboat travel some one once remarked that "a fatalistic attitude was a good travelling companion."

The following is an account of the *Moselle* steamboat disaster published in the *Cincinnati Daily Evening Post*, Thursday April 26, 1838.

AWFUL STEAMBOAT DISASTER

Yesterday afternoon, between five and six o'clock the most shocking occurrence we were ever called upon to record, took place in this city. The new and elegant steamboat *Moselle*, under the command of Captain Perin, left the wharf, bound to St. Louis. She had on board then upwards of two hundred passengers. This is the opinion of those who were present, and had the best opportunity of knowing from their constant attention on the wharf, and had habitual intercourse with the boats coming to it. She passed rapidly up the river to near the corporation line, where lay several rafts loaded with emigrants, whom she took on board. The rafts, and the neighboring shore and street, were covered with people, many of whom were drawn there by curiosity, others to take farewell of their departing friends. The moment they were all on board, with their effects, and while the kiss of affection was yet warm upon their lips, and the closely pressed hand had not yet recovered from the pressure it received at parting, the boat blew up, and in a moment not less than a hundred and fifty souls were ushered into eternity, while others, horribly scalded and mangled, survived to die a lingering death. At five o'clock this morning, we went to view the scene of destruction and horror. We saw the mangled remains of from fifteen to twenty and spent an hour in learning from neighbors such particulars as they witnessed themselves. A young woman who saw the explosion, in common with many others, remarked that "It rained human bodies and fragments of bodies." Some were blown to the distance of two and three hundred feet, while others fell near the spot from whence they ascended; one fell upon the roof of a house, which he passed through until stopped by his shoulders, he was not quite dead when removed, but he died in a few minutes. Captain Perin and nearly all the officers of the boat, are among the victims. We never saw such an illustration of the power of steam, a part of one of the boilers was thrown a distance of 100 yards, and crushed the pavement where it fell; another large piece of a boiler was thrown against a buidling on the hillside, back of a tan yard, and not less than two hundred yards from the boat—it totally demolished the gable end of the building; another heavy piece fell about fifty feet from the building near a vat, where five men were at work a few minutes before. Numerous instances are

The United States Engineer snagboat *E. A. Woodruff* was a steel-hull craft, built in Charleston, West Virginia. She began operations in June 1876. The *Woodruff* was a side-wheeler, and carried a crew of forty. Her task was to remove the many snags and wrecks in the Ohio River. At a later date, she was fitted out with a steel "polly hook" used for the removal of sunken coal barges. The *Woodruff* discontinued snagging operations in 1921, and was then used to accommodate workmen engaged in the construction of a dam.

She was named after Lieutenant Eugene A. Woodruff of the United States Engineers who died of yellow fever at Shreveport on September 30, 1873. He had been working at snag removal on the Red River and volunteered to assist the sick and dying during a severe epidemic. (From the collection of the Public Library of Cincinnati and Hamilton County.)

mentioned of the distances to which things were thrown, which would surpass belief, but for the known veracity of those who saw them. When the explosion took place many who were on the hurricane deck ran aft and jumped into the river, and were drowned. An old lady, who was in the ladies cabin, with whom we have conversed, says she was thrown down, and the partition between the two cabins fell upon her, which saved her; her son perished, and she lost all her effects. She remarked, she could not realize it, and it was evident from her conversation, that she did not. Having progressed thus far, we went out to see if we could not learn some further particulars. All we have been able to add, is that a dead body has been found in Kentucky, having been blown the entire breadth of the river. It was remarked to us, by numbers of those who saw it, that great as were the fragments of human bodies, as well as of the boat and her cargo, that fell upon the shore, they were trifling when compared with those that fell in the river. There is great difference of opinion as to the number on board, varying from two hundred and twenty five to three hundred and upwards; the latter number is insisted upon by many who saw the boat explode. We are unable, after much exertion, to give names of the sufferers, or the saved and will not name when we are not certain. The number saved, from every information we can obtain,

does not probably, much if any, exceed fifty. Consequently, not less than a hundred and seventy five have perished. The boat is the most perfect wreck we ever saw from any cause. Since the above was in type, we learn that the body of the man thrown into Kentucky and recovered today, was that of the pilot, Mr. Jas Gleaning.

One of the greatest of all steamboat catastrophes was that of the *Sultana*. In the dead of night on April 27, 1865 her whole battery of boilers exploded when she was a few miles north of Memphis. Unfortunately, the Mississippi River at that point was almost fifty miles wide. Demolition of the levees on both sides of the river during the Civil War had caused all the bottom lands to be inundated, making rescue attempts extremely difficult. The *Sultana* had 2,200 troops aboard, some of whom were on their way home from prison camps along with some 200 civilians. A newspaper of the day stated, "For weeks afterwards the Mississippi was strewn along its shore with stark mangled bodies, lodged in the crotches of trees, caught horribly in the undergrowth of willows and cottonwoods. According to the best figures available, 647 persons per-

**The twin steel hulls of the snagboat *Chas. R. Suter*
under construction in 1886.**

Engaged in the construction of a lock and dam on the Ohio, above Maysville, Kentucky the towboat *Jim Wood* shoving a tow of empties upstream, stalled and drifted on to a mooring pin, submerged by the unusually high river level. All attempts to dislodge her failed and with the river level falling the pin punctured up through the hull. While attempts were being made to lift her off, the current swung her around to face downstream and in the process added a huge gash to her hull. This photograph was taken November 14, 1917 shortly before demolition commenced. It illustrates the extreme flexibility of the wooden hull. (Courtesy of S & D Reflector, from the files of the Hunting District, U.S. engineers.)

Snagboat *J. S. De Russey.*
(From the collection of the Public Library
of Cincinnati and Hamilton County.)

ished." One surviver related that while clinging to a log with three others, one man committed suicide rather than endure the agony caused by the freezing water. Nine men survived when the section of the boiler deck on which they were sleeping hit the water intact, they clung to their improvised raft as it floated off to safety.

Insurance as applied to the river paddle steamers is an enormous subject in itself, upon which one could expound at great length. As with all new ventures risks were either over- or underestimated. A general pattern of practice never did evolve until just before the steamboat era closed. Insurance premiums on the vessels would be quoted for specific periods of the year, sometimes one month at a time, and they varied according to the season and river. The quality of the crew, the age of the vessel and state of the machinery were also factors to be considered in the coverage. The improvements made in steamboat design and the progress in improving safety by the engineers in taming some of the dangerous stretches of the rivers, would also be relevant. Premiums were often as much as one third of the value of the vessel. Some owners preferred to take the chances of loss rather than pay the rates asked The condition of other boats was such that they were refused coverage at any price. In order to discourage careless handling or intentional destruction, it was the usual practice to limit liability to below that of the boat's value, although some owners did obtain full coverage by insuring with more than one company. Because of the poor maneuverability of the early stern-wheelers they were considered a greater risk than side-wheelers, and for a time were uninsurable. The cargo was usually insured separately, the expense falling on the shipper. The rates varied with the length and type of trade.

Throughout history, imaginative reporters have embellished basic facts with their own interpretation to build a tailor-made mystery, all of which makes excellent copy for a gullible public. In most instances lack of witnesses and material evidence, plus the passage of time, prevented any worthwhile investigation to disprove their argument. Some of the most bizarre mysteries concerning paddle steamers were believed to have been cover stories for insurance frauds when lack of evidence, either by accident or design, prevented anyone proving otherwise.

8

SHOWBOATS

"Showboat a comin'" was the sound which echoed down the river banks as a popular medley of the time was heard from its distant calliope. Colorful posters pinned to trees, fences and barns announced its arrival. On the big day, its presence was proclaimed by raucous tootlings of its steam calliope which echoed around the river valleys. The larger showboats often boasted a brass band which would parade round the town; a noisy, but effective way of announcing its arrival. For nearly a century the showboat brought plays, music, recitations and vaudeville to the river towns and villages. Evening performances were marked by the fiery splendor of oil flares mounted on tall poles, which illuminated the path leading down the bank to the showboat's gangplank and led the theatregoers straight into the box office. They would then file into the ornate auditorium to be entertained by an orchestra until the curtain rose. The season, starting in early spring ran into late autumn, extending even longer

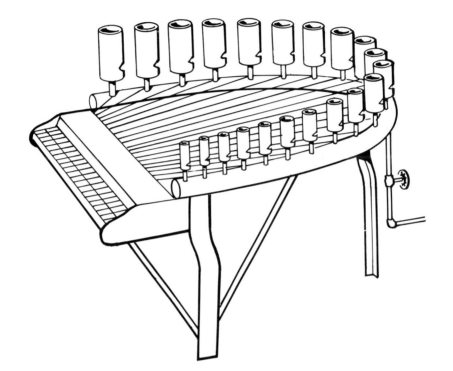

The Calliope, (a cally-ope or steam pianna) is one of the rarest and most unusual instruments ever to come on the American scene. This colorful collection of whistles, pipes and valves in which steam is forced through a series of tuned whistles, is controlled through a keyboard. Its music is harsh, although the word calliope, derived from the Greek, means "beautiful of voice." A Vermont farmer, Joshua Stoddard of pawlet, Vermont, takes credit for its invention in 1855, he originally intended his "American Steam Piano" to replace church bells that summoned worshippers. The notion never caught on however, so he introduced his instrument to the steamboat in 1856. The first steam calliope of which any record exists was fitted on the *Unicorn* in 1858. Others claim that the *Excelsior* had the first but it was also reported that this calliope's fame was short lived—it was silenced after the noise gave the Excelsior's captain and some of his passengers a headache. One boat, the *Armenia*, which operated on the Hudson River until about 1870, carried a 34 whistle calliope, but the instrument had to be modified because it sapped the boat's power, preventing it from sailing under full steam. It quickly became standard equipment on the more luxurious steamboats and showboats of the period. When the showboat calliope opened up, the effect was inescapable, its raucous notes could be heard for miles around, it also drowned out the bands of competing showboats. With a full head of steam, the sound given the right conditions, could carry up to nine miles away. It was generally situated on the top deck of the showboat and supplied with steam piped from the towboat, or in rare instances from its own special boiler. In its off duty hours its pipes also distilled drinking water.

farther south. The first showboat was nothing more than a barge with a barn on top, fitted out with wall-to-wall benches and a small raised area which served as a stage. Showboats were occasionally constructed on old steamer hulls. Some were self-propelled but the space required for machinery reduced the already limited space, making it commercially impractical. If they lacked engines they were towed (pushed) by paddle steamers, but control was usually held from the pilot house of the showboat, with bells and tiller lines connected by cables between the boats. It was a family of English actors named Chapman who started this era. Their

The showboat *New Sensation*—one of a series of five operated and owned by Captain A. B. French. Showboat crews/performers had to be versatile to "keep the show on the road." A classic example of this was in the many talents of Captain French's wife Callie, who began as mate, cook and housekeeper aboard the *New Sensation* in 1878. She progressed to pilot, captain, vocalist and tightrope walker, doubtless continuing as cook, housekeeper, and feminine lead in the more serious dramas. (From the collection of the Public Library of Cincinnati and Hamilton County.)

showboat was nothing more than a crude barn built on a barge which measured 100 feet long by 16 feet wide, and it was constructed in Pittsburgh in 1831. A shallow stage with muslin-drawn curtains, and candle footlights stretched across the stern. The seating consisted of board benches, without back rests or cushions, securely fastened to the floor. Living quarters occupied the bow. The plan was to drift with the current down the Ohio and the Mississippi, stopping for one night performances at each river landing where an audience seemed likely, and in late winter at the end of the season, sell or scrap the boat in New Orleans. Should the venture prove to be successful and profitable the Chapmans would return to Pittsburgh, build another boat and repeat the trip the next year. On

reaching a settlement they hired a town crier to proclaim their performance, and posters nailed up in prominent positions outlined the program. It usually listed a full length play, followed by a monologue, impersonations, sketches, music and singing. Later Chapman Showboats were towed by a steamboat. An admission charge of fifty cents for adults, was often beyond the pocket of some would-be patrons, so it was not unusual to accept meat, vegetables or any other produce in season to cover admission. As more entrepreneurs entered the field, the respectability of the showboat diminished and in consequence, some showboat arrivals were met by groups of armed citizens inviting the theatre to keep moving. No lady would be seen to set foot on board. In 1878 however, a man by the name of A.

The *Floating Circus Palace*, with an overall length of 200 feet. The arena was forward on the main deck, which also contained 1,000 cane bottom chairs in the dress circle. The family circle in the first gallery seated 1,500 on cushioned seats and the second gallery provided space for 900 negroes on benches, a total capacity of 3,400. Off the main circus arena was a museum of "curiosities and wonders," as well as dressing rooms for the performers and stalls for the horses. The museum boasted over 100,000 "curiosities" and included stuffed animals, figures in wax and sideshows. The boat printed its own daily newspaper, *The Palace Journal*, distributed free of charge to both the patrons and performers. The print shop

and the editorial desk were also located in the museum and many visitors no doubt found the printing of the newspaper as interesting as the other curiosities. During her first year the *Palace* was towed by the stern-wheeler *North River* and later by the powerful *James Raymond*. The towboat *James Raymond* also contained a small theatre called the "Ridotto" which presented dramatic performances, vaudeville, minstrel entertainments and concerts by the boat's twelve-piece brass band. Music in the main arena was provided by a large pipe organ. A chime of bells mounted on the hurricane deck provided free concerts for the riverside crowds that the boat's appearance usually attracted.

B. French restored the reputation of showboats when he built an eighty-nine seat floating theatre called the *New Sensation*. His shows comprised every type of variety entertainment of the day, and he insisted that ladies be admitted. Along with the popularity of the showboat, the boats themselves became more luxurious. Seating was made more comfortable, fully stocked bars were fitted and the quality of the shows improved. The exact number of boats operating is not known, but by 1900 less than thirty operated on the rivers, and this figure was to drop below ten by the late 1930s. The popularity of the showboat declined with the arrival of the car, and the birth of the cinema. There was a fleeting resurgence in 1926, with the publication of Edna Ferber's novel *Show Boat*, later produced as an operetta and then as a film. It required a lot of people to keep a showboat "on the road," and most performers had two jobs—that of actor and crew member. Even the captain/pilot would have a leading role when the curtain rose. As a general rule the actors' accommodations would be located on the forward end of the theatre's second deck, but the kitchen and dining room were back on the towboat.

Some showboats have survived, most of which are permanently moored in some of the larger towns, and have become tourist attractions. One of the larger and most luxurious showboats to run on the rivers was the 200-feet long *Goldenrod*. It was 46 feet wide, with a seating capacity of 1400. It was fitted out with a steam heating system, electric fans for summertime cooling, and "2,500 incandescent lights, arranged in attractive patterns," as the advertisements read, the electricity being generated on the *Goldenrod*'s towboat. The interior of the showboat was carpeted, and full-length mirrors mounted in brass frames adorned the walls which were decorated in gilt and red velour. The *Goldenrod* now rests on a steel barge moored on the St. Louis River front. Designated as a national historic landmark she stages theatrical productions by St. Louis groups.

One of the most outstanding showboats of all time was the *Floating Circus Palace*. Its overall length was 200 feet, with a seating capacity of 3400: about one-third in the dress circle and the remainder in the two galleries. A wax museum was located in the stern, as were the dressing rooms for the performers and stalls for forty horses. The company numbered about one hundred and were accommodated on the upper decks. The steamboat which pushed the *Palace* also contained its own small theatre for dramatic performances. Both boats had gas lighting, a novelty itself at the time. The group brought regular circus acts to the river towns from 1851 to 1862, when the *Palace* entered the Civil War and was confiscated by the Confederates and used as a hospital boat.

The showboat was born to take entertainment to frontier families. When the frontier vanished the showboat died.

9

RACING

Two paddle steamers racing along, neck and neck, quaking, straining and groaning from stem to stern, was a sight to quicken the pulse of any observer. Black smoke and sparks belching from their tall stacks, white steam spouting from the top of their scape pipes and the boiling white froth being thrown out from the churning paddle wheels fading into long streaks trailing behind as the boats sliced their path through the water, presented a colorful, action-packed, never-to-be-forgotten scene. Racing provided a spectacular and exciting diversion for the steamboat traveler, but like the legendary professional gambler it has traditionally been given more publicity than it deserved. Major races staged over long distances were few in number, but minor impromptu contests were frequent and nonetheless thrilling for both passengers and crews alike. Some races were prompted by the need for a newcomer to gain publicity. Others were purely commercial since the first boat at the landings would skim the cream of freight and passengers at the expense of the boat following. To many passengers it was the thrill of a lifetime, a talking point for years afterwards, but others did not share this excitement and sought safety by putting the maximum possible distance between themselves and the boilers. As with all forms of transport, speed was the essence in the battle for business on the rivers, and to the fastest went the honor of "holding the horns." The horns were a guilded pair of deer antlers, a symbol of the speed king, usually mounted on the pilot house or in an even more prominent position.

Stories surrounding these races are many and varied, owing little to truth, while the crew's efforts to win knew no bounds. All was fair in love and steamboat racing. Boats were trimmed to give the best possible speed by the removal of cargo and spares. Highly combustible fuels were used, such as bacon sides, turpentine, pitch and pine knots. The machinery was tuned to the peak of condition; fueling barges were picked up en route, then towed alongside as they were frantically unloaded, and then cast adrift. Some engineers were even known to tie down the safety valve. This kind of dangerous behavior forced up insurance rates, but even leg-

The *Baltic* and *Diana* racing on the Mississippi in 1858. From the lithograph of a painting by George F. Fuller. (From the collection of the Public Library of Cincinnati and Hamilton County.)

Lithograph of the race between the
Natchez and the *Robt. E. Lee*. Actually,
the boats were never as close together
during the race as they are shown in
this and many other prints. (Courtesy;
Missouri Historical Society.)

islation failed to stop it. Apart from the thrill of the chase, it was enjoyed by passengers and the riverbank crowds alike. It was good for business, an excellent sales gimmick. Towboats even raced to reach the locks!

Credit for the most famous steamboat race of all time was shared by the *Rob't E. Lee* and the *Natchez* in 1870. A business rivalry between Captain J. W. Cannon of the *Lee* and Captain T. P. Leathers of the *Natchez* started it all. Although they denied any intention of racing, behind the scene they made preparations for the inevitable event. The captain of the *Lee* stripped her of unnecessary weight and made provisions for refueling from barges en route. The two boats were evenly matched although the *Natchez* was slightly larger. The race began at five o'clock in the afternoon of June 30, from the New Orleans levee, the *Natchez* leaving about four minutes behind her rival. From the onset the *Lee* drew steadily away from the *Natchez*. By the time the *Lee* had reached Memphis, the halfway point, she had stretched the lead to one hour. Fog encountered above Cairo, Illinois caused both boats to reduce speed and the *Natchez* was further delayed by engine trouble. The *Lee* arrived at the finish line at St. Louis at 11:25 a.m., July 4. The record-breaking trip had taken three days, eighteen hours, and thirty minutes. The *Natchez* arrived some six hours later. Arguments about the race, which continued for many years centered around a controversial refueling when the seamer *Frank Pargourd* was lashed to the moving *Lee* to unload a hundred tons of pine knots.

10

The outbreak of the Civil War had a dramatic effect on the steamboat. Initially the rush to move cargo and passengers from the north to the south and vice-versa created good business. But it was followed by an almost complete shutdown with scores of steamboats lying idle at the wharves of the principle river cities, the former busy levees abandoned and deteriorating. Although General Grant used boats in the winter of 1862 to capture Fort Donelson, a year or more passed before the armies realized the full value of the steamboat as a troop and supply transport. This demand grew until it in turn created a shortage of suitable vessels. So great was the demand in fact, that paddle steamers eight-years and older, normally destined for the breakers, were sold at prices close to their original cost and caused a spate of new steamboat construction. This after almost all the available boats had been commandeered by the military, primarily in the north, but to a lesser degree in the south. There were times when more vessels were chartered than could be fully employed, and some lay idle at the wharves for days while others were used for storage purposes or to house officers.

The steamboat, designed to operate without the need for shore facilities when loading and unloading cargo, was particularly suitable for the army's transport needs. The boats could be brought ashore anywhere and could disembark troops, horses, wagons and stores directly on the riverbank. This rapid action could be taken without the need for wharves or any other terminal facilities normally associated with moving large quantities of men and equipment. A landing such as this also contained the element of surprise. The war created another variation of the paddle steamer: Vessels

A. O. Tyler. **This gunboat was one of three pioneer gunboats in the United States fleet. She was a con-** verted river steamer. (From the collection of the Public Library of Cincinnati and Hamilton County.)

were fitted with slanting wooden casements to enclose the gun deck, machinery and paddle wheels; the casements were then clad with steel sheets. They were called either "tinclads" or "ironclads" depending on the thickness of the steel. Other changes introduced when converting to a tinclad were the lowering of the boilers and steam pipes to a less exposed position in the hull, structural reinforcement of the hull, and the plating of the pilot house and other exposed places with sheet iron. Their armament usually consisted of six or eight light cannon. In some rivers convoys were formed and advanced under the protection of tinclads. Because the south had little iron the Confederate navy used two heavy timber bulkheads with compressed cotton bales between them as their armor. Needless to say, these earned the nickname "cottonclads."

U.S.S. Mound City, ca. 1863. An "ironclad" built at Mound City, Illinois. 175 feet long, 30 foot beam. She took part in the battle of Saint Charles on the White River in Arkansas June 1862. She suffered 140 casualties from scalding and drowning when a Confederate shore battery scored a hit on her boiler. This in spite of her 122 tons of steel plate armor. (From the collection of the Public Library of Cincinnati and Hamilton County.)

Sybil, a "tin clad" of the Civil War. (From the collection of the Public Library of Cincinnati and Hamilton
County.)

INSIDE THE WOODEN CASEMENT PROTECTING THE GUN DECK

Possession of the Mississippi Valley was of great strategic importance during the war, as its vital resources were essential for victory. Thus some of the most active and decisive phases took place in this area. Paddle steamers had a major role in one of the most important battles of the Civil War, centered around Fort Henry on the Tennessee River and Fort Donelson on the Cumberland River. At the onset of hostilities in the Mississipi Valley, Kentucky and Missouri remained neutral, and Union forces had control of the Ohio River Valley. Confederate armies established fortified strongholds on the rivers in Tennessee, Mississippi and Louisiana. General Grant decided that the key to ultimate victory "in the west" lay in the control of the Mississippi, but in order to achieve this aim it was first necessary to subdue Fort Henry and Fort Donelson. These fortifications served both to bar the southward advance of the Union army and protect the flanks of the Confederate positions. On February the 4th 1862, Grant with 15,000 men aboard river transports started up the Tennessee River. The convoy was escorted by three wooden gunboats and four Ironclads. Grant's plan was to move directly on Fort Henry from the east side of the river as General Smith was mounting a land attack on Fort Heiman on the west side. The gunboats meanwhile were to go up river and lend support to Grant's landborne attack. The fleet poured accurate and devastating fire on the fort. The onslaught by the gunboats was so intense that the Confederate commander of the fort surrendered to the flag officer of the fleet before Grant's army arrived. Grant, flushed with the success of the operation, decided without delay to mount an attack on Fort Donelson. The transports with their gunboat escort steamed back down the Tennessee and up the Cumberland River. The attack began on February 14 when the fleet advanced on the fort with the ironclads spread across the front and the three wooden gunboats supporting them in the rear. The gunboats commenced firing at a range of one and a half miles, continuing the barrage to within 300 yards. They were met with accurate return fire, all the gunboats were hit and suffered damage. The following day Fort Donelson surrendered. This time the combined efforts of Grant's troops from the landward side and the gunboat barrage had determined complete victory. Over 12,000 men surrendered to the Union forces. Grant's army fighting its way south occupied Nashville nine days later.

Chattanooga, a Civil War gunboat. Photograph was taken on the Tennessee River during the Civil War. She was built by Federal troops who gave her the nickname of "Chicken Thief." (From the collection of the Public Library of Cincinnati and Hamilton County.)

The advance of the railroads, prior to this period, was not necessarily always an advantage in moving troops, since it required large numbers of troops to protect the miles of track, bridges, viaducts, crossings, etc. Traffic on the river however was almost completely safe as the inaccurate fire from shore batteries was of little consequence. Thus, large numbers of troops could be moved in complete security. In several instances major expeditionary forces were transferred to their objectives by the river fleets. The Union forces which under General Grant ascended the Tennessee River to Pittsburgh Landing in the spring of 1862 were carried to the battlefield of Shiloh by an immense fleet of 153 steamboat transports. In the winter of 1862–1863 a fleet of some seventy-odd vessels carried an army of 40,000 troops, including cavalry and artillery, to participate in Sherman's attack on Vicksburgh having traveled some 475 miles from Memphis.

In April of 1862 during the Civil War, Union forces had occupied the City of New Orleans, the gateway to the Mississippi. Having this important city occupied by the enemy was a bitter blow to the Confederates, but defiantly they refused to resign themselves to the fact that they had lost control of the great river. Operating out of secret bases located up the tributaries of the Mississippi, they fought back with piratical raids on both enemy ships and positions. For over two years the Union forces suffered these increasingly embarrassing attacks, but in March of 1862 Command headquarters decided that action must be taken to destroy this impudent force. Acting on information received from spies that the enemy base was located in the Shreveport area on the Red River, headquarters gave Admiral Porter the task of drawing up plans for an attack on the base, which comprised a few forts, supply depots and shipyards. He evolved a plan; it was ambitious and risky. He planned to sail a battle fleet up the Red River and with support from a land force pick out the enemy piecemeal. The Admiral's plan was approved and a river fleet was assembled at New Orleans. It comprised 19 ships, 14 of which were armored. Meanwhile an armed force of 30,000 men was being organized under the command of General Banks who was to direct the land operation. In retrospect the appointment of Banks was a mistake; he had

little confidence in the plan and his lackadaisical attitude resulted in an ill-prepared army. By the end of March the fleet was ready to sail but the Admiral was informed that the land force still lacked both ammunition and wagons. An outraged Porter sent for General Banks, but he was not available—he was visiting friends, showing no enthusiasm to his appointed task. Meanwhile the preparations for the expedition had not gone unobserved by Confederate spies, who reported back to their leaders. The expedition set sail and met the land force at Alexandria. By this time Confederate scouts already on the look out, were able to send accurate reports back to their headquarters. The Confederate commander, on being informed of the arrival of the fleet, viewed the scheme with some amusement, remarking that "they must be mad sailing up the Red River at this time of year." He judged the enemy venture hazardous and intended to turn it to his advantage. Finally, on the 3rd of April the amphibious expedition left Alexandria bound for Shreveport. On the way up river they destroyed a few abandoned shipyards and forts, but there was no sign of Confederate troops. A messenger from General Banks reported that the General's force also had not established contact with the enemy. The Admiral ordered the fleet to continue upstream. Two days later however the crews noticed that the water level was below that anticipated.

The Admiral was not aware that this was no trick of nature; the Confederates' scheme to ground the fleet by damming off all the tributaries feeding the Red River was having its effect. The Union fleet's first indication of the seriousness of the situation came when the *Osage* went aground in the middle of the river. Meanwhile, General Banks had continued his advance without making contact with the enemy, but his progress was being followed by Confederate scouts. Banks's force ran straight into an ambush at Sabine Cross Road, withering fire from the surrounding hills marked the commencement of a furious battle. Well aware of his hopeless situation he had little choice but to order a retreat. They withdrew to a hill only to find that they were now surrounded by the enemy. While this battle raged other Confederate forces launched an all out attack on the stranded *Osage*, they were about to board her after suffering heavy losses when the gunboat *Lexington* suddenly appeared, sailing

The completed dam.

The *Essex* leading the fleet in its bid for freedom.

cautiously over the shallow waters. Under the heavy crossfire from the two ships, the Confederates hastily withdrew. Admiral Porter, unaware of either the whereabouts of General Banks's force or its fighting state, decided that the fleet had to seek deeper water. The fleet turned about to steam for Alexandria. Banks had extricated his army from the trap and began his retreat toward New Orleans, completely abandoning his part of the expedition. It was not long before Admiral Porter found himself in a similar situation. The Confederates anticipating Porter's move had prepared an ambush at Mount Alexandria. His fleet came under fire so intense that a bullet actually singed the Admiral's beard. Although the fleet seemed to be sailing out of danger the situation suddenly took a turn for

the worst when the *Eastport* struck a mine and the Admiral had to order the crew of the *Cricket* to abandon ship when she was knocked out of action. A further two support ships were to be lost before the fleet cleared the ambush. The remaining ships finally managed to reach the waters of Alexandria, but it was immediately apparent that the water was too shallow for the ships to clear the rapids. A possible solution was put forward by a Colonel Bailey to construct a dam upstream of the rapids and, providing they could hold out until the river level rose, cut through the center of the dam and sail the fleet out on the crest of the wave, over the rapids and into safe waters. The plan was risky and full of problems but in the desperate situation the only alternative was to abandon the ships and

Cairo, a sister ship of the *Mound City*. She was blown up on December 12, 1863 on the Yazoo River. Her guns and pilot house were recovered in 1961.

(From the collection of the Public Library of Cincinnati and Hamilton County.)

make their way back to New Orleans over land. A working party under Colonel Bailey immediately set to work cutting down trees, and the rest of the army deployed itself to defend the area until the task was completed. They beat off several Confederate attacks and it became a dramatic fight against both time and the enemy. The work went on without let up until the dam was complete, and within two days the water rose sufficiently to allow the fleet to move around freely. The next problem was how best to cut the dam to create the wave essential to success. It was decided that explosives were too risky, they might just damage the dam causing it to disintegrate slowly. There was only one answer—it had to be cut by hand, but the chances of the men appointed to that task surviving the rush of water were very slim, and they had no chance whatsoever of regaining the safety of the boats. In spite of the suicidal nature of the task, a group of volunteers stepped forward and began the tricky undertaking. At the critical moment the fleet was signalled and Admiral Porter in the *Essex* led his

ships line astern through the gap. The fleet sailed down over the rapids on the rush of water, and headed for the Mississippi which they reached on the 21st of May, making New Orleans a few days later. None of the brave volunteer party who cut the dam survived. This tragic venture became known as the Red River Fiasco.

"Ram fleets" were created from commercial steamboats, the bows being reinforced and ballasted. Mortar boats constructed on flat barges were towed into position and moored when required. It was not unknown for blazing rafts to be pushed toward the enemies fleet to burn them out of the water.

The commercial value of steamboats reached a peak in the years preceding the Civil War. During the conflict most civilian shipping ceased, and when the war ended and the boom conditions were gone the real decline of the steamboat began. The railroads had already made big inroads into the lucrative passenger traffic.

11

he years between 1850 and 1860 were often referred to as the golden age of the steamboat. However the national transport pattern established by the steamboat, based on the natural inland waterways had obvious limitations. The principal purpose of the early railroads was usually to feed or connect steamboat lines, but the appearance of the railroad in the Mississippi Valley heralded the end of the steamboat era.

Railroad construction began around 1830 with only 23 miles of track. By 1840 a further 2,800 had been added. By 1850, track in excess of 9,000 miles had been laid and it linked most of the important river cities. By 1860 the railroad was nosing its way along the banks of the Mississippi, and the network tracks exceeded 30,000 miles. No longer was progress tied to the river, tracks were laid to suit traffic requirements. The next decade took the track miles up to 53,000 and by 1880 a massive 93,000 miles had been

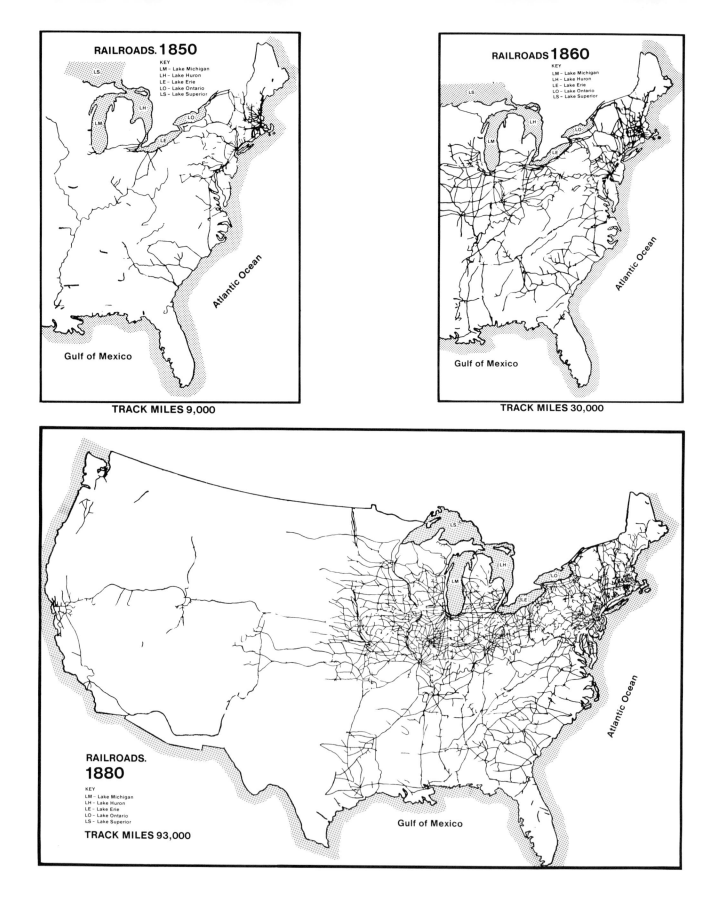

RAILROADS. 1850

KEY
LM – Lake Michigan
LH – Lake Huron
LE – Lake Erie
LO – Lake Ontario
LS – Lake Superior

Atlantic Ocean

Gulf of Mexico

TRACK MILES 9,000

RAILROADS 1860

KEY
LM – Lake Michigan
LH – Lake Huron
LE – Lake Erie
LO – Lake Ontario
LS – Lake Superior

Atlantic Ocean

Gulf of Mexico

TRACK MILES 30,000

RAILROADS.
1880

KEY
LM – Lake Michigan
LH – Lake Huron
LE – Lake Erie
LO – Lake Ontario
LS – Lake Superior

TRACK MILES 93,000

Atlantic Ocean

Gulf of Mexico

laid. Rail passengers could now travel from the Atlantic right through to the Pacific. The railroads, not subject to the vagaries of the weather and the state of the river levels, were able to maintain fast and regular schedules, pushing the frontiers further west, overrunning the steamboat territory. Initially the railroad only skimmed off the passenger traffic; it was still cheaper to move freight by steamer where the river routes served the requirements. A reduction in railroad freight charges brought about by a combination of better equipment and improved efficiency still further eroded the steamboat markets. By 1880 the steamboats were fading into the past. In their final attempt to survive they were relegated to towboat roles, pushing groups of barges loaded in the main with coal or timber.

Stern-wheeler *John Quill* receiving freight from an electric railway. The *John Quill* built in 1907 operated on the Mobile, Tombigbee, Worrior and Alabama rivers until 1928 when she was dismantled. (Courtesy, S & D Reflector, photo Murphy Library.)

12

FAMOUS PADDLE STEAMERS

The *Belle of Louisville*

She began life as the *Idlewild*, built by James Rees & Sons, Co., Pittsburgh. Launched in late 1914, she was 157½ feet long, 36 feet wide and 5 feet deep and could attain a speed of ten miles an hour. Not large by the standards of the day, the *Idlewild* joined a huge fleet of similar vessels. However, the crowd who witnessed her launching would not be aware that she would be among the last of a line going back some one hundred years. The experience gained over the years made her one of the safest and most economical boats on the rivers. This without doubt contributed to her survival. She is now known as the *Belle of Louisville*, and is run as an excursion boat out of Louisville, Kentucky.

The *Idlewild* first operated as a ferry and day packet, carrying passengers and freight (mostly farm produce and livestock) for the West Memphis Packet Co. When all-weather roads became practical in the early twenties the competition from oars and lorries became so severe that the packet side of the business closed and she became an excursion boat. In 1928 she was sold to the New St. Louis & Caloun Packet Corporation of Hardin, Illinois. After a season as a New Orleans excursion boat she went to St. Louis to work the Illinois river transporting produce along with and between excursions. In 1931 she was put out to charter to the Rose Island Co., after the loss of their boat the *America*. In 1934 she was at Louisville as an excursion boat. Her rugged construction was beneficial when, in World War II, she towed oil barges for the defense program. After the war she returned to the excursion trade and in 1947 she was bought by J. Herod Gorsage, of Peoria, Illinois, and was renamed *Avalon*. The following year saw another change in ownership when she was purchased by Mr. E. A. Meyer, of Cincinnati, Ohio. As the steamer *Avalon* she tramped the rivers steaming to such far-flung ports as Omaha, New Orleans, Minnesota, Pittsburgh, Illinois, Nashville, and all points

Building the hull of the *Idlewild* in the autumn of 1914 at Pittsburgh.

The *Idlewild* at Madison, Indiana in the 1930s.

An eighteen-foot model of the *Idlewild* seen here on her trials, August 1981. Constructed based on plans supplied by A. Lawrence Bates of Louisville, Kentucky. A twelve-volt battery powers two wheelchair motors, the drive is taken through two reduction sets to a layshaft. Cranks mounted on the ends of the layshaft transmit the action to the paddle wheel shaft cranks through the pitmans. Switchgear enables two speeds ahead and two speeds astern to be selected, maximum speed is about 4 m.p.h. The hull is of fibre-glass sandwich construction with "bluebord" forming the core. Three pine keels fibre glassed in run the full length of the hull. (Photograph by Rodger Wagstaff.)

The *Avalon* near Pittsburgh in 1955.

The stern-wheeler *Avalon* at the public landing, Marietta, Ohio, ca. 1950. The building left of center is the Hotel Lafayette, a popular meeting place for steamboat buffs. The town also houses the Ohio River Museum, devoted to the history of the Ohio River, emphasizing the steamboat era.

The *Belle of Louisville* at Cloverport, Kentucky.

between. 1958 was the beginning of the end for the *Avalon* when she hit a lock gate at Emsworth Dam. She was carrying a crowd of some 1130 railroad fans, many of whom were thrown on to the deck. The resulting law suits and the years of deferred maintenance costs drove Meyer into bankruptcy in 1962. At that time the *Avalon* was purchased by her current owners, Jefferson County and the City of Louisville. Within two months work commenced on her restoration. She was renamed the *Belle of Louisville* and to this day operates out of Louisville as an excursion steamer. She is also the center for banquets, meetings, concerts and dances. Her restoration was the subject of a book by Alan L. Bates, the architect employed to supervise the work. The book, *Belle of Louisville* also covered her past history. A little more excitement is added to her life when she enters the annual steamboat races competing for the coveted "Guildered Antlers." Even before her first name change structural alterations and additions were taking place on the *Belle* and indeed each time a new photograph appeared one wondered if it was the same beat. The major final alteration came when ten feet were added to her foredeck. Although she was originally fueled by coal she now runs on oil, and consumes about one hundred and fifty gallons an hour when under way. The *Belle* has been designated a Kentucky landmark by the Kentucky Heritage Commission, adding to her worldwide fame.

Poster advertising the *Avalon*.

The *Belle* was designated a Kentucky landmark, another laurel added to her worldwide fame.

The *Betsy Ann*, 1899.

The *Betsy Ann*

A steel-hulled vessel, built in 1899, she measured 185 feet overall with a beam of 33 feet. Her draught varied between three and five feet depending on the load. From the waterline to the top of her chimneys she measured fifty-one feet. In her regular "trade" she operated as a packet boat between Natchez and Bayou Sara on the Mississippi. Noted for her catering she also boasted a famed "Betsy Ann Brand" of mint juleps. Also of note was her distinctive whistle said to be not unlike the soft sound of a nightingale. The *Betsy Ann* was also a mail boat and had a post office on board. In her latter days she was operated on the Ohio River by a new owner, Captain Frederick Way, Jr. He wrote the *Betsy Ann* based on the log kept during his ownership from 1925 to 1929. In it he gives an account of a trip of 150 miles on one cylinder with a full load. The port pitman (connecting rod) had parted company with the crosshead and as a result the piston pushed out the cylinder head. The boat, in river terms, had "run through herself."

A friendly rivalry existed between the *Betsy Ann* and a boat of similar size called the *Christ Greene*.

Many times this rivalry showed itself in a race to the next port. In 1928 a newspaper reporter, short of news, witnessed one such contest from the river bank. This insignificant event was totally misreported, blown up out of all proportion with a mixture of assumptions and unsupported "facts." It resulted in the press provoking an official race between the two boats. The race was of short duration, lasting only two hours and fifteen minutes, and was allegedly won by the *Christ Greene* with a two minute lead. The result of the race as with many others was long contested. Tens of thousands of people turned out to see the two smoking stern-wheelers paddle along at the breathtaking pace of eight miles an hour. By any standards it was the most exciting event on the Ohio for many years.

In the spring of 1932 the *Betsy Ann* was converted into a towboat and she continued in this role until 1940 when she was dismantled. She was last heard of in 1948 when her hull was sold to a boat club on the Meramec River.

The *Delta Queen*.

The *Delta Queen*

The steamer *Delta Queen* has been described as a "heritage that can be touched." She has the air of royalty. Yet the *Delta Queen*, last of the authentic steamboats, continues to make history today as she carries her colorful tradition along the rivers. This vessel's elegance is unequalled. Teak handrails line the decks; stained glass windows decorate the lounges and many staterooms. She glistens with crystal chandeliers, brass fittings, and ceiling beams of oak and mahogany. Her lounges are finished with satin drapes richly upholstered sofas and wing chairs, and deep carpeting. She was first assembled on the River Clyde in Glasgow, Scotland, where she was built in prefabricated pieces, which were later shipped to Sacramento Bay for reassembly and launching at Stockton, California. In 1926 regular cruises between Sacramento, Stockton, and San Francisco were begun. During World War II, the United States Navy pressed the *Delta Queen* into service as a yard ferryboat to transport troops and wounded across San Francisco Bay. In 1946 she was purchased by Captain Tom Greene of Cincinnati's Greene Line Steamers. Moving the *Delta Queen* to the Mississippi River System was a feat many said couldn't be done. Captain Greene had the shallow draught boat towed across 5,000 miles of open sea; down the Pacific coast, through the Panama Canal and across the Gulf of Mexico to New Orleans. From there the steamer traveled upriver under her own power to Pittsburgh, to be re-outfitted for passenger service. This historic voyage was the subject of a book by Frederick Way, Jr., entitled *The Saga of the Delta Queen*.

A new era in the life of the *Delta Queen* began on June 3, 1948, when she embarked on a round-trip cruise between Cincinnati and Cairo, Illinois. Since then the steamer has faithfully plied the Mississippi and Ohio Rivers calling at such ports as New Orleans, St. Louis, Louisville, Cincinnati Pittsburgh, Natchez, Vicksburgh and, as would be expected, Hannibal, Missouri, the home of Mark Twain. Because the *Delta Queen* is such an authentic, fully restored steamboat and is one of the few remaining links with a vital era in American history, she was entered in the National Register of Historic Places on June 15, 1970. Although, through the years, the *Delta Queen* has carried statesmen, Supreme Court judges and celebrities, the *Queen* gained worldwide recognition as a one-of-a-kind vacation when President Carter spent a week on board in August of 1979. She has accommodation for 188 passengers and is manned by a crew of 77. She is 285 feet long with a beam of 58 feet, and draws 7½ feet of water. Her overall height is 55 feet, measured from the waterline to the top of her single, hinged stack. She is powered by condensing steam engines with oil fired water-tube boilers, propelled by a twenty-nine feet diameter paddle wheel, eighteen feet wide. This combination propels her galvanized steel hull to maximum speed of twelve miles per hour. Her cruising speed is around seven miles per hour. Since 1947 she has continued to cruise more than 30,000 miles annually, visiting more than 14 states, from her home port in Cincinnati, Ohio.

The Delta Queen, is an anachronism that by "progressive" and "current" thinking should probably not even exist in this supersonic age. In fact, she is only back in her rightful place on the river due to the efforts of a band of determined enthusiasts. In 1966 two disastrous fires on cruise ships—the *Viking Princess* and the *Yarmouth Castle* (neither of American registry)—prompted Congress to enact a "Safety at Sea" law that specified that all American flag-flying ships, with overnight accommodations for more than 50 persons, would have to be constructed of fireproof materials. Although the *Delta Queen*, with accommodations for 192 passengers did have a steel hull, her four-deck superstructure was fashioned of teak, oak, mahogany, walnut and ironwood and in consequence fell foul of the provisions of the new regulations. Operating on America's vast river system she was never out of sight of land but this did not deter lawmakers. They no doubt were influenced by the abysmal safety record in the early days of steamboating. Boats blew up with alarming regularity, or they were snagged on underwater obstructions and sank, or they simply shook themselves to pieces. Most

A new wheel for the *Queen*. While cruising the Ohio River below Louisville in August 1980, a passenger idly gazing over the stern, suspected a fracture in the paddle wheel shaft. The chief engineer confirmed the trouble and the boat was landed. When the stern-wheeler *Delta King* (a sister ship) was taken out of service some years ago, her paddle wheel shaft was stored "just in case." The photograph shows the rebuilt paddle wheel on the *Delta King*'s old shaft being installed. The assembly weighs some forty-four tons, and when the damaged paddle wheel was removed the stern of the *Delta Queen* rose four inches. Rebuilding the wheel took nearly a month, but the *Queen* maintained her schedule with the aid of the towboat *Imogene Igert*. She pushed the *Queen* facing a barge lashed alongside the port stern quarter. (Courtesy S & D Reflector, photo by Dr. Lou Haase.)

owners regarded themselves fortunate if their craft survived five years of operations. Boats were pushed to their limits by the intense competition and hazardous waters. No authoritative casualty figures for the early days of steamboating exist, but one esimate claimed that between 1840 and 1850, over 4,000 persons were killed or injured in steamboat accidents. In contrast over the past eighty years they have had a perfect safety record. The last passenger who perished in a fire was an inebriated gentleman, who, because of his unsociable behavior, was locked in his cabin to sober up. In his drunken stupor he tried to register a protest by setting fire to the cabin and died in the inferno. The flames soon consumed the boat but the 1,200 passengers aboard escaped without injury when the pilot made for the shore before the fire took hold. In 1966 the *Delta Queen* was operated by the Greene Line—a company with a faultless safety record. In eighty years of operating a total of twenty-eight boats on America's rivers not one life was lost to fire or accident on any of the line's steamboats. But the ill-defined wording of the law wouldn't budge. The *Queen* was given two two-year extensions by special Congressional bills and then all further legislation became stymied.

With time running out, in November, 1970 friends rallied to the *Delta Queen*'s defense. The signatures on the many petitions organized to influence Capitol Hill revealed that just about everybody wanted this important piece of river history saved. Thirteen governors joined Congressional representatives in a massive lobby to keep her afloat. National historical groups explored every possible avenue to preserve the *Queen*. Their efforts must have had the desired effect, for an estimated quarter of a million persons wrote their legislators to voice their support. Twenty-five separate bills, most asking for a permanent exemption to the unjust law, were introduced only to come to an abrupt halt at the desk of the Chairman of the House Merchant Marine and Fisheries Committee. He stubbornly bottled up each bill and refused to bring them to the floor for a vote. Not to be out-maneuvered, the *Queen*'s defenders took a new tack: they found an unobtrusive bill, and promptly attached a rider to it that granted the *Queen* yet another extension to keep her steaming. This time it made the floor of Congress and was passed happily, by a huge vote,

295 to 73. The Senate approved the decision and the bill was sent to the White House for the President's signature. Once the legislation was signed, the company acted on its promise to upgrade the vessel. She was dry-docked and the work commenced immediately. In 44 years of operations on the Sacramento, Mississippi, Ohio and other rivers her hull had worn thin in a few spots. Hundreds of riverbank landings, plus the dents and abrasions suffered in the normal day to day operations had taken their toll, so much so, that nearly one fourth of her hull plates had to be replaced. Removal of the 44-year-long accumulation of paint, exposed rare and long forgotten mahogany and oak woodwork, plus fine brass and bronze castings. The woodwork was in many cases, just refinished, sealed and left unpainted, so that its natural beauty could be appreciated. Likewise the unpainted metal was buffed up and meticulously polished. Although her original equipment included fire hydrants, a fire alarm system and a complete sprinkler system, other improvements had been added over the years and during the refit even more safety devices were incorporated. An improved fire detection system was installed, and fire retardant paint was used extensively throughout the boat. An important and significant step towards higher standards of safety was the installation of new electric pumps for the fire and water mains. The installation of a diesel powered generator enabled the main boilers to be shut down when in port, the main generators being powered by steam. Numerous other minor improvements were incorporated during the refit, and she sails, with an exemption from the Safety of Life at Sea act, until 1988.

The Cincinnati-based Delta Queen Steamboat Co. traces its roots in river history back to 1890. It was in this year that Gordon C. Greene, Inc. was founded by Captain Gordon Christopher Greene, to operate packet steamers on the Ohio and Mississippi Rivers. The company flourished and was renamed Greene Line Steamers, Inc., Gordon's sons, Christopher and Thomas, followed in their father's footsteps as the Company's successive managers. It was Tom, who in 1947, twenty years after his father's death, and three years after the untimely death of his brother Christopher, purchased the *Delta Queen* and brought her to Cincinnati. Refurbished

Steamer *Gordon C. Greene* formerly the *Cape Girardeau.* Ran in the Ohio river trades, retired from service in 1949. She was then converted into a floating museum-restaurant, and moored at points in Kentucky, Florida, and New Orleans. The boat was moved to Hannibal, Missouri in 1962 and re-christened the *River Queen.* Her final mooring was the St. Louis waterfront, where she sank in 1967, and was then broken up. (From the collection of the Public Library of Cincinnati and Hamilton County.)

at a cost of three-quarters of a million dollars, Tom, his wife Leatha, and his mother Mary began sailing the *Delta Queen* in style and comfort along the Mississippi and Ohio Rivers in 1948. When Mary and Tom passed away in 1949 and 1950 respectively, Leatha assumed responsibility of the line until the sale of the operations in 1973. Between 1973 and 1976 the *Delta Queen* was owned by Overseas National Airways, who changed the Company's name to the Delta Queen Steamboat Co. It was under the direction of Overseas National Air-

ways, that construction on the world's largest and most spectacular paddle wheeler ever, the *Mississippi Queen* was begun. Ownership of the *Delta Queen* passed into the hands of Coca-Cola Bottling Co., of New York in 1976. In the spring of 1980, the Delta Queen Steamboat Co., was spun off from the Coca-Cola firm. Today, the Company not only continues as the publicly-owned operator of America's only overnight passenger steamboats, but has also registered outstanding profits during the 1982–1984 period.

The *Mississippi Queen*

On July 25, 1976, as the culmination of a gala bicentennial celebration, the steamer *Mississippi Queen* was commissioned at Cincinnati, Ohio. The ceremony marked the end of a ten-year sequence of planning, design and construction of this majestic steamboat. It also marked the beginning of a new era in American travel as the *Mississippi Queen* joined her sister, the legendary *Delta Queen*, in carrying adventurous travelers along the broad waters of the Mississippi River system. The Delta Queen Steamboat Co. management conceived the building of a new paddle-wheeler because of successive, near-capacity years of operation by the *Delta Queen*. The intent from the outset was to build the largest, most spectacular riverboat ever, and the massive undertaking was made possible by the work of many fine craftsmen. The exterier was devised by James Gardner of London, designer of Cunard's *QE II*. The interior design was the work of the internationally known Welton-Becket and Associates of New York. Builder of the *Mississippi Queen* was Jeffboat, Inc., of Jeffersonville, Indiana, where more than 4,800 steamboats were built in the nineteenth century. Although her exterior lines emulate steamboats, from the previous century, and she boasts the traditional steam-powered paddle wheel and boistrous calliope, all similarity to her predecessors ends there. From the start, the *Mississippi Queen*'s design, including an all-steel hull and superstructure, captured the ultimate in

luxury and comfort for the twentieth-century cruise passengers. At a final cost of twenty-seven million dollars, she offers her guests the convenience of elevators, a swiming pool, sauna and gym, a beauty shop, a movie theatre, elimate control throughout with individual controls in each passenger room, and a complete, telephone and public address system. But the majestic steamer has not lost touch with her heritage. Brass trim, hand-blocked zinc paneling, brilliant mirrors, steel and brass parquet dance floors and plush carpeting throughout recall the opulence of the great steamboats of the past. Sailing under the American flag with an all-American staff and crew, the *Mississippi Queen* cruises the year round. From New Orleans in the south and Minneapolis/St. Paul in the north, she carries her 396 passengers along 1700 miles of the Mississippi River, showing them the vast and varied panorama of America in unequalled style. Manned by a crew of 142, she is 382 feet long, with a 68 foot beam and draws 8 feet of water. Her height, leadline to the top of her twin telescoping stacks, is 80 feet 9 inches. Her all-steel hull is pushed along by a four cylinder, horizontal, tandem compound condensing steam engine and automatic oil-fired boilers. The engine drives a paddle wheel 22 feet in diameter, and 36 feet wide. Her average cruising speed is 8 miles per hour but she is capable of reaching 12. In an average season on the Mississippi her mileage exceeds 30,000.

The *Mississippi Queen.*

The *Natchez* (number eight) at Vicksburgh, Mississippi, loading cotton and seed for New Orleans.
(From the collection of the Public Library of Cincinnati and Hamilton County.)

The Stern-Wheeler *Natchez*

The *Natchez*, (the ninth) was named after a long line of ships which have traveled the Mississippi waters since 1823. She is owned by the New Orleans Steamboat Company, a subsidary of the Lake George Steamboat Company of New York, was the first commercial stern-wheeler built in the United States in the last half of the century and was the first all steel river steamboat completed to meet the requirements of the Safety at Sea Law. Completed and christened in 1975, she has a top speed of 17½ miles per hour. She operates out of New Orleans, has a crew of 35, and can carry up to 1,600 passengers.

Designed by Alan Bates of Louisville, Kentucky the *Natchez* is 285 feet long with a 44 feet beam. the *Natchez* is built like the old Mississippi steamers and the boilers and drive assemblies date back over fifty years. Most of the propulsion equipment comes from the *Clairton*, which was built for United States Steel in 1926 and pushed coal barges on the Monogahela River. Her tandem compound condensing engines, fifteen and thirty inches in diameter by seven foot stroke, operate on two hundred and fifty pounds steam pressure. The *Natchez* most closely resembles the old Mississippi stern-wheelers *Virginia* and *Hudson*. It features an antique, all copper steam whistle that was formerly on a tugboat owned by Jones & Laughin Steel Corporation. The clarion bell, which is inlaid with two hundred and fifty silver dollars to improve its tone, once belonged to the *Queen City*, and the calliope was specially designed and built in Cincinnati for the *Natchez*. The main bar, which is unusually long, is the only wooden item on board.

The earliest of these *Natchez* vessels was built in New York City in 1823 and burned at New Orleans in 1835. In 1838, planters and merchants in Baltimore built another boat of the same name; this one sank in 1842. Captain Thomas P. Leathers of Cincinnati built and operated the next series of eight boats that are commonly considered the *Natchez* boats today. The first one of this series was built in 1854 and traveled every Saturday from New Orleans to Vicksburgh. Sold in 1848, the boat was abandoned four years later. The next *Natchez*

vessel constructed in 1849, also ran the Vicksburgh course, then changed to a route that took her from New Orleans to Fort Adams. The boat was sold and sank in 1866, in Mobile Bay. The next *Natchez* carried bales of cotton during its ill-fated career on the river. She collided with the steamer *Pearl* in 1854 and eight lives were lost when the *Pearl* sank. The next month, February, the boat was burned in a wharf fire at New Orleans, killing Captain Leathers's brother. The burned boat was rebuilt and became the forth *Natchez*, but she too was burned in 1859. *Natchez* number five, which carried the machinery from *Natchez* number four, also carried cotton, but was taken over by the Confederates at the beginning of the Civil War to be used as a troop transport boat. On March 13, 1863, she was sent up the Yazoo River and took fire about twenty-five miles beyond Yazoo City, Mississippi— all forty-three passengers survived.

The next boat was the famous *Natchez* which entered the great race against the *Robert E. Lee* in 1870 (see p. 172). The race, filled with controversy, resulted in a win for the *Lee*, but the *Natchez* has recently regained its pride. In 1975 and 1976, in the first stern-wheeler races since 1870, the *Natchez* soundly defeated the *Delta Queen*.

Natchez number seven was built in 1879 and featured skylight glasses on which were twenty-two Indian portraits. The boat was later tied up because of lack of business, and two years later, in 1889, she sank near Lake Providence, Louisiana. Though attempts were made to salvage the boat, it eventually broke in two. Natchez number eight, a stern-wheeler, was built in 1891. At the age of eighty, Captain Leathers was killed in a bicycle accident in New Orleans and his widow, Blanche Douglass Leathers, obtained a master's license and took over the boat. This boat had several accidents, however and was purchased at a U.S. Marshal's sale in New Orleans in 1915 by Captain W. A. Duke, who operated her until 1918 when she was dismantled. A twin-screw towbeat named *Natchez* was built in West Virginia in 1920 and served as a "city boat" until she came to a tragic end on a Greenville, Mississippi bridge in 1948, killing thirteen people.

When the new *Natchez* was christened in 1975, a plaque was presented by the shipyard, designating the new boat as the official "*Natchez* Number 9." Designed to preserve all the beauty and romance of the early giants of the Mississippi, the *Natchez* is also a prime example of modern shipbuilding and technical superiority. Passengers aboard the *Natchez* can enjoy life on the Mississippi just as it used to be but in an atmosphere of luxury and convenience.

The *Natchez*.

The *Rob't E. Lee*

The steamer *Rob't E. Lee*, the most famous river steamboat of all time, was built at New Albany, Indiana in 1866. Her hull design was a masterpiece of carrying capacity and speed. She was a "6,000 bale" boat designed to carry that quantity of cotton without obstructing the boiler deck passengers' view. She cost more than $200,000 to build—a fortune in 1866. The *Rob't E. Lee* was typical of the finest class of steamboats of her day and was a truly remarkable machine. She was very fast, easily capable of exceeding twenty miles per hour in still waters and yet she could carry enormous loads on a draught of only seven feet. She had two main engines, the cylinders of forty-inch diameter had a ten-foot stroke. At that time they were the largest high pressure engines on the river. Steam provided from a battery of eight boilers also pow-ered three fire pumps, a unique and major safety factor in this all wood boat. She was built to run between Vicksburgh, Mississippi and New Orleans, Louisiana but in lean times made trips from New Orleans to St. Louis, Missouri and Louisville, Kentucky. The highlight of her career was the great race she had with the *Natchez*, billed as the biggest sporting event of 1870. She arrived in St. Louis six hours ahead of the *Natchez* having covered the 1,218 miles from New Orleans in three days, eighteen hours, and thirty minutes.

The *Lee* boasted sixty-one state rooms in her main cabin, with an additional twenty-four passenger cabins in the texas. A nursery provided accommodation for children and their nannies. The carpet in the main cabin measured 222 feet long by 17½ feet wide, a Royal Wilton Velvet made to

**The *Rob't E. Lee.*

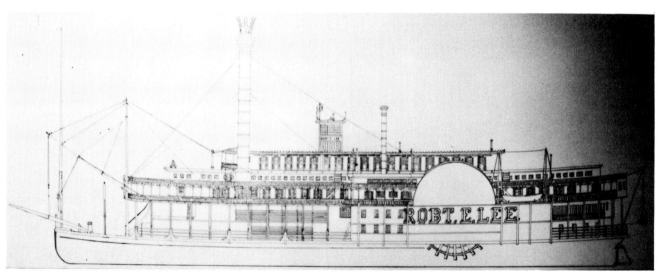

The *Rob't E. Lee*. Probably the best photograph of the "racer" *Lee*. (From the collection of the Public Library of Cincinnati and Hamilton County.)

order in a single piece. Her opulent main cabin was garnished with dazzling chandeliers suspended from arched and fretted ceilings etched with gold. Stained glass skylights, immense mirrors, the Royal Wilton carpet, the pure zinc white of the sides, the rosewood stateroom doors and the imitation Egyptian marble sills, all combined to make it bear an appearance of oriental luxury and splendor never before seen floating in the wild waters of the rivers. The solid rosewood furniture artistically and elaborately carved included twenty extension tables each of which could seat twelve guests, and still had ample space for extra side tables. After a remarkably smooth life, the *Rob't E. Lee* was dismantled in 1876; much of her outfit and equipment was used in building a new and bigger *Rob't E. Lee*. The hull became a wharfboat moored at Memphis, Tennessee. Various fittings and furniture did however find their way into museums and some into the hands of private collectors. Her dazzling chandeliers light the Presbyterian church at Port Gibson, Mississippi. Her boilers were salvaged and installed in a sugar mill at Bush Grove Plantation on Bayou LaFourche, Louisiana. They served until 1922 generating steam for drying sugar. Her successor known as *Rob't E. Lee II*, built in 1876 burned near Vicksburgh in 1882, with a loss of twenty-one lives.

13

THE LEGEND LIVES ON

The rapid development of paddle steamers opened up an epoch which in our time can only be paralleled by the progress of air travel. The scale of this travel revolution is beyond the imagination. It was an age in which the rivers became highways, giving access to vast areas of unexplored, undeveloped land. It was a time when the paddle steamer disgorged its cargo of pioneers and their goods into a vast, sparsely populated, wild, and uncivilized world. Is it any wonder that the Americans hanker for this historically rich period of their grandparents as portrayed in old prints of river life? The sheer numbers of paddle steamers depicted in such illustrations only served to show the steamers' far-reaching significance in the everyday life of riverside communities. It was a collection of vast commercial enterprises spreading their tentacles up every river and creek wherever the shallow draught steamers could freely navigate. A steamer's whistle eerily echoing around the hills was akin to the call of the pied piper. Its strident tone drew the populace to the levee, there to be enchanted by the feverish activity surrounding a boat's arrival. It was a social occasion, with a frenzied interchange of passengers and cargo, gossip and news. All this was accompanied by a backdrop of hissing steam, smoking stacks and powerful machinery, to be fully enjoyed before the curtain came down as the boat departed and the levee reverted to its original serene state. Is it not understandable that in our high speed, chrome and plastic world, enthusiasts, and to a lesser degree the general public, hanker after such a panorama?

Alarmed by the demise of this once great fleet, steamboat enthusiasts, individually and collectively, are trying to salvage some part of the paddle steamers' golden age before it disappears forever. Action, activated by nostalgia has resulted in many such boats being saved from the breakers. They are being converted into floating museums, theatres or restaurants, and memorabilia is painstakingly sought to furnish them authentically. Smaller craft are readily converted into floating homes. Purpose-built diesel-engined paddleboats designed for local day cruising are becoming increasingly popular. These craft add a new dimension to the life of the city dwellers turning the clock back to Mark Twain's childhood, and allowing them to live out a microcosm of the nostalgic golden age of the paddle steamer. River lore narrated by the present-day guides only serves to enhance the memories of ancestor's tales. All this nostalgia is played out with background music provided by the threshing paddle wheel. Even without such nostalgia what could be more satisfying than quietly rolling along such rivers as the mighty Mississippi, through misty valleys and the lush verdant wilderness of the northwest territory? Curiosity holds fast; there is no anticipating the river, islands, creeks, wildlife, wild flowers and cascading waterfalls round each bend. On a larger scale, purpose-built steamers such as the *Delta Queen*, the *Mississippi Queen* and the *Natchez* cater to the top end of the market. Accommodation to modern standards, and onboard entertainment, allows passengers to enjoy the atmosphere in safety and comfort. The voyages lasting a week or more, are remote from the high speed concrete ribbons that criss cross the country. They open up a new panorama to be absorbed at the leisurely pace of the paddle steamer. Self evidently, the legend lives on.

The *Becky Thatcher*, formerly the *Commodore*, built in 1967 and now operated by the New Orleans Steamboat Company. She is licensed to carry 400 passengers. (Courtesy of New Orleans Steamboat Company.)

The *Valley Gem*, a 98 passenger day cruise stern-wheeler. Owned and operated by Captain James E. Sands, out of Marietta, Ohio, cruising the Muskingum and Ohio Rivers. (Courtesy of Captain James E. Sands.)

The stern wheel diesel *Cotton Blossom*, built in 1974 operated by the New Orleans Steamboat Company, New Orleans, an excursion boat for local cruising, licensed for 350 passengers. (Courtesy of New Orleans Steamboat Company.)

The *Betsy Ann*, owned by River Entertainment Incorporated, Chicago, designed strictly for parties with no sleeping quarters or galley. The *Betsy Ann* is a luxurious stern wheel riverboat operated on Chicago's lakefront. It was conceived for partying in a style which has not been seen in Chicago since the late 1800s. An authentic, paddle-wheel driven, all-steel boat, 110 feet long with a beam of 23½ feet she has a top speed of 13 knots. She has a maximum capacity of 450 passengers, but her normal load is usually around 215. Her paddle wheel is in two sections each independently driven by hydrostatic motors. Two 671 GMC diesel engines hydraulic pumps provide the power. The paddle wheel arrangements allows for better maneuvering, which can be a problem on stern-wheelers. (Courtesy; River Entertainment Inc., Chicago.)

The *Mark Twain*. A 150 passenger excursion boat. Steel hulled with two stern-mounted padddle wheels, chain driven and powered by a 150 H.P. diesel engine. Built at Dubuque, Iowa by the Dubuque Boat and Boiler Co. in 1962, 85 feet long by 22 feet. She was originally named *Lady M*, then owned by River Excursions, Inc., Dubuque, Iowa. The Great River Packet Company purchased her in 1975 and operated her out of Hannibal, Missouri. She then made another move to Covington, Kentucky having been purchased by B & B Riverboats. (It is reported that she is to be leased out to Captain Rainboult, former pilot on the *Delta Queen*. He has plans to operate from Vicksburgh, and to rename her *The Spirit of Vicksburgh*.) (Courtesy; Captain Bob Lumpp, Great River Packet Co.)

The paddle steamer *Minne Ha Ha II*, a mountain steamboat, completed in 1969, steel hulled, 103 feet long, 30 foot beam, draught 3 feet, 6 inches, speed 7 miles per hour. Designed as a day-tripper, operates on Lake George, New York. The engine room is surrounded by glass panels enabling passengers to watch the equipment operate and the engineer respond to the bell signals from the pilot house. *Minne Ha Ha* means "laughing waters" and was given to the wife of the famous Indian chief Hiawatha. (Courtesy; The Lake George Steamboat Company, N.Y.)

Glossary

Acorn. An ornament used as a finial on masts and booms, etc.

Antlers. Deer antlers were the symbol of speed supremacy in the steamboat world. A speed contest was referred to as a race for the horns.

Ash pan. The space under the boiler grates where cinders and ashes collected.

Ash well. A pipe from the ash pan through the bottom of the boat, discharging into the river.

Backing bell. A jingle bell hung on a spiral spring. Used for signalling the engineer.

Balance bucket. A heavy bucket plank in the paddle wheel used to balance the weight of the crank and pitman.

Balanced rudder. A rudder with part of its area forward of the tiller post where pressure exerted by the water flow assists the pilot turn it.

Bars. Low-lying riverbed elevations of sand, gravel or rock as obstacles to navigation.

Bateau. A big flat-bottomed skiff capable of carrying an entire family.

Bayou. A secondary waterway or an intermittent watercourse, chiefly in the lower Mississippi basin.

Beam. The width of the hull.

Bell rope. The rope line leading from the bell pull in the pilot house to the bell in the engine room or the bell on the roof.

Bell stand. A wooden stand just aft of the pilot wheel where the bell pulls were located.

Bitts. A pair of upright posts with a cross bar used for tying lines.

Boiler deck. The deck above the boilers, which supports the cabin and staterooms, or the second deck.

Boneyard. Usually a river location where worn out steamboats awaited the wreckers.

Boom. The pole carried at or about a forty-five degree angle between the deck and the derrick from which the stage is suspended.

Brake. A device used to hold the pilot wheel, especially when the boat was backing, (going astern) and the wheel due to pressure on the rudders was likely to run wild. Operated by a foot pedal.

Breast board. The lower board used for closing the front of the pilot house.

Bridle. A device used for holding the pilot wheel in one position while the pilot tended the stove or got a drink etc.

Broadhorn. A flat boat, so named from the two large sweeps projecting from each side.

Brow board. The adjustable visor over the pilot house front, the upper board for closing the front.

Buckets. The blades of the paddle wheels, sometimes referred to as floats.

Bull rails. Pine or poplar planks inserted between the stationaries along the outboard sides of the main deck, set in slots so that they may be easily removed when necessary.

Bustle. A bulge in the stern rake caused by building the rudder depressions.

Butterfly. A piece added to the top of a rudder to increase its area.

Cabin. The interior portion of the boat on the boiler deck. It contains the main saloon and staterooms.

Cabin arch. A fanciful bracket used to carry the cabin ceiling and one source of the term "Steamboat gothic."

Calliope. A tuned set of whistles with individual valves and a brass piano style keyboard for operating them. A form of steam organ.

Capstan. An upright winch used for pulling lines.

Chain. A rod used to prevent decks from sagging or hulls from hogging.

Chains. A term applied to a succession of rod bars or ledges.

Cotton packet. A side or stern wheel boat, modified to carry cotton with an extra wide main deck, and a very narrow boiler deck and cabin.

Crossboard. A large wooden 'X' painted white. Usually fastened to a tree at the waters edge, so placed to assist pilots by marking the channel. (Sometimes called a daymark.)

Cross chain. A system of wrought iron rods used for holding up the guards.

Cut off. A short new channel formed when a river cuts through the neck of an oxbow bend.

Cylinder timber. A long structural member which supported the engine cylinder and the paddle wheel bearing.

Dead man. A large baulk of timber with a cable attached around its center, buried on the river bank to provide an anchor point on which to warp the boat.

Death hook. A hook on the extreme end of a safety valve lever where the engineer could hang weights to increase the steam pressure.

Dip. The distance the paddle wheel buckets extend into the water.

Doctor engine. An auxilliary engine used for running pumps. Its use made it possible to shut down the main engines at landings or whenever needed.

Dollar hole. A tube in the steamboats kitchen through which garbage was dumped into the river, so called because wasteful cooks often threw good food into this device, at the owners' expense.

Draught. The amount of hull extending into the water measured vertically.

Duckpond. The space in front of a towboat and behind the tow and flanked by the drivers.

Fantail. The deck outboard of the cylinder timber and aft of the hull.

Fathom. A depth measurement of six feet.

One fathom is termed	mark one.
Two—	mark twain.
Three—	mark three.
Four—	mark four.
No bottom—	above mark four.

Fender. A device used to prevent boats and hulls from chafing against other objects.

Fire box. The room where the fireman stands.

Finial. A decorative top to a pole or beam. Can take the form of an acorn or similar carving or turning.

Flank. To back the stern away from the intended direction the boat is to go.

Free loaders. Passengers on a steamboat, who by virtue of being relatives or regular shippers, claimed free passage (sometimes referred to as dead heads.)

Freedmans bureau. A section of the texas reserved for colored passengers traveling first class. Found in boats on the southern trades, usually, and sometimes quite elaborate.

Gangplank. A plank used to span the gap between the boat and the shore or boat to boat. When suspended from above it becomes a stage.

Government light. A beacon maintained by the government. Illuminated by oil lamps, later by electric light. Usually colored white, green or red. An invaluable aid to pilots at night.

Guards. The portion of the main deck extending over the sides of the hull.

Gunny sack. A strong coarse sack, made from jute.

Guy. Any line used to hold a boom or mast or smokestack firmly in place.

Hog chains. Wrought iron rods, from one to two and one-half inches in diameter used to hold up the ends of the hull, supported on wooden posts.

Hull inspector. A term used as a nickname for a bad snag in the steamboat channel on the river.

Hurricane deck. The upper deck of a steamboat.

Ice Gorge. With a severe "freeze-up" on the river the ice formed was sometimes of great thickness. When it broke up and moved, it frequently gorged against obstructions and in narrow and crooked channels, a single gorge so formed could be miles in length and many feet high. When such a gorge moved, its force was irresistible, sweeping everything before it.

Jackstaff. The flagpole at the bow of the boat. The pilot took sights along it in steering the boats course.

Jockey bar. The spreader bar between the cylinder timbers at the ends aft of the paddle wheel. Also applied to the bar between hog chain braces.

Keelboat. A craft constructed of heavy planks with planked ribs like a ship. Sharp at bow and stern, and although of light draught they could carry from twenty to forty tons of freight. Called keelboats because of the heavy four-inch square timber that extended from the bow to the stern along the bottom of the boat.

Kevel. A two-horned deck fitting, a cleat.

Lazy bench. The bench in the pilot house where everybody but the pilot sits.

Lead line. A length of line to which a lead weight is attached to sound out depths. The cord usually marked off into fathoms (six feet).

Levee. A sloping or graded wharf sometimes paved.

Main deck. The first deck, it supports the boats machinery and boilers, it is also used for cargo stowage.

Marine ways. A set of parallel rails, broadside on to the riverbank. Fitted with wheeled cradles on which boats were lifted out of the water for inspection and repair.

Mark twain. A twelve foot (two fathoms) depth sounding.

Monkey rudders. Auxilliary rudders on each side of the main rudders gives quicker response in steering.

Navy jack. A flag consisting of the field only of the American flag, i.e. that portion on which the stars are mounted.

Nighthawk. A bulbous device on the jackstaff which was used by pilots at night to ascertain indistinct shorelines.

Oxbow. A U-shaped river bend where only a narrow neck of land remains between two parts of the stream.

Packet. A river steamboat designed to carry freight on it decks, and passengers, the latter usually accommodated in cabins located on the upper deck.

Pirogue. A large canoe often forty or fifty feet long, from six to eight feet wide, and capable of carrying a family and several tons of household goods. On the Missouri it could also describe two canoes about six feet apart with a platform built between them.

Pitman. The connecting rod between engine and paddle wheel cranks.

Planter. A "snag" which has one end firmly fixed in the riverbed and stands in a nearly vertical position.

Quarter twain. A thirteen and a half foot depth of water.

Rake. An angle of inclination.

Reef. A ledge or shelf in the river bottom.

Ripple (or ruffle.) See shoals.

Roof bell. The signal bell located on the roof or upper decks. Used to announce departures, fog warnings, and fire and boat drill alarms.

Rosettes. Circular cast iron ornaments bolted to woven wire railing fabric.

Roustabout. A deckhand working under the mate, doing any task assigned to him. Job usually associated with Negroes.

Scape pipe. Exhaust stack for expelling steam.

Shipping up. A term used to describe the act of shifting the cam rod from the lower pin on the reversing lever to the upper, or vice versa.

Shoals. A series of sand or gravel bars over which water descended with a greater than normal slope, also called a ripple.

Skiff. A small rowboat.

Sounding pole. A depth gauge for use in shallow waters, up to eighteen feet in length. Marked off in one foot sections. Each section painted alternately red white and blue.

Stacks. Another name for chimneys.

Stage of the river. The level of the water is called the stage, i.e. pool stage is when the river is at normal level behind a dam. Flood stage is when the river rises to a theoretical level dictated by the U.S. Engineers where damage begins to occur.

Stationaries. The vertical timbers rising from the edge of deck to support the boiler deck above.

Texas. The cabin situated on the skylight roof.

Texas deck. The topmost deck below the pilot house. It became known as the texas, according to a contemporary explanation, probably because it was annexed.

Torch basket. A wrought iron basket on a long pole, used for burning wood thus making light for nighttime navigation. Used on steamboats before the days of searchlights.

Trades. A field of steamboat operations between two ports.

Up the hill. Anywhere out of sight of the river, is "up the Hill."

Verge. The aftermost mast on the boat.

Wharfboat. A floating warehouse/office, moored to the bank. Usually located in the larger towns. Invariably built on an old steamboat hulls.

The Ohio River Museum. Located at Marietta, Ohio, houses a special section on steamboats, in addition to tracing the history of the Ohio river. Many fine detailed models of famous steamboats are on display alongside posters, paintings, photographs and such items of memorabilia as steamboat whistles and steamboat furnishings. On display outside is a replica of a flatboat, and moored alongside on the banks of the Muskingum River is a real paddle steamer now in retirement, the *W. P. Snyder Jr.* In 1955 she was acquired by the Ohio Historical Society, a gift of the Crucible Steel Company of America. It is open to the public mid-April to November.

Riverboat Museums and Associations

Some Museums and Libraries with river sections of interest to the paddle wheel enthusiast.

Campus Martius Museum, Marietta, Ohio.

Cincinnati & Hamilton County Public Library, Eighth & Vine streets, Cincinnati, Ohio.

Fred W. Woodward Riverboat Museum, Dubuque, Iowa.

George M. Verity. (Steamer) Keokuk River Museum, Keokuk, Iowa.

Golden Eagle River Museum, Bee Tree Park, St. Louis, Missouri.

Howard National Steamboat Museum, 1101 East Market Street, Jeffersonville, Indiana.

Mariners Museum, Newport News, Virginia.

Mississippi River Museum, Mud Island, Memphis, Tennessee.

Missouri Historical Society, Jefferson Memorial Building, St. Louis, Missouri.

Missouri River History Museum, Brownville, Nebraska.

Monon Center River Museum, Greensboro, Pennsylvania.

Murphy Library, University of Wisconsin, La Crosse, Wisconsin.

The Ohio River Museum, Marietta, Ohio.

The Paddle Steamer Preservation Society, United Kingdom.

Smithsonian Institute, Washington, D.C.

The Steamship Historical Society of America, Inc.

The River Museum, Wellesville, Ohio.

Lilly Library, Indiana University.

Associations.
American Sternwheel Association, Inc.
Sons and Daughters of Pioneer Rivermen.

The steel-hulled towboat *W. P. Snyder Jr.* approaching the west end bridge on the Ohio River, Pittsburgh, ca. 1945. Now a permanent exhibit at the Ohio River Museum, Marietta, Ohio. (From the collection of the Public Library of Cincinnati and Hamilton County.)

Notable Dates

1736 John Fitch's *Philadelphia* boat, with a steam engine driving vertical paddles.

1765 The keelboat comes into use on American rivers. Birth of Robert Fulton.

1785 The flatboat comes into use on the western rivers.

1790 Mike Fink starts his career on the rivers.

1792 Elijah Ormsbee builds a small steamboat using "ducks foot paddles."

1800 The Natchez Trace becomes a crude road.

1801 Publication of *The Navigator* the first serious attempt to publish a river guide.

1807 Fulton launches his *Clermont*.

1810 New York State grants a patent to Fulton and Livingstone, giving them sole rights to navigate the rivers of that state by steamship.

1810 Pittsburgh shippers send a force down river to clear out the "Cave in Rock" robbers.

1811 The first steamboat on the western rivers, the *New Orleans* left Pittsburgh for Cincinnati at eight miles per hour.

1815 Robert Fulton's death.

1816 Captain H. M. Shreve pilots the first mechanically successful steamboat, the *Washington* down the Ohio River.

1824 Enactment of the River and Harbour Act.

1829 Shreve launches his snagboat *Heliopolis*.

1830 Railroad track miles total twenty-three.

1832 The source of the Mississippi, Lake Itasca, discovered by Henry Rowe Schoolcraft.

1833 Captain H. M. Shreve sets out to break up the "Red River Raft."

1852 Enactment of the Steamboat Inspection Act.

1855 Joshua Stoddard, a Vermont farmer, invented the steam calliope.

1860 Railroad track miles reach 30,600.

1861 Start of the American Civil War.

1865 The 'Sultana' explodes at Memphis; 1,647 lives lost.

1870 Famous race between the *Natchez* and the *Rob't E. Lee*.

Railroad track miles reach 53,000.

1871 The Federal government began to issue river reports.

The peak year for paddle steamer construction, one hundred and fifty-five recorded launchings.

1873 The first Federal dredge went into operation.

1875 Ohio river steamer *General Lytle* revolutionizes nighttime navigation with the introduction of the electric arc searchlight.

1877 The stern-wheeler *Chouteau* (a rebuild on the hull of the *Carondelet*) one of the first boats to be fitted with electric lights.

1880 Government river charts become available. Railroad track miles reach 93,000.

1881 Steamer *Henry Frank* carried 9,226 bales of cotton, a record.

1882 Steamer *Joseph B. Williams* makes a record tow of 26,000 tons of coal. The Edison electric light system fitted throughout on the U.S. mail steamer *Kate Adams*, the first steamer to be so fitted.

Paddle Steamers
in Philately

Cover commemorating Robert Fulton's steamboat
Clermont which depicts the inventor Robert Fulton.

Limited edition of cover commemorating the twenty-fifth anniversary of the *Snyder's* arrival in Marietta on September 16, 1955 when her engines were last rung off as an operational towboat. She now is permanently moored to the banks of the Muskingum River in Marietta as a primary exhibit of the Ohio Historical Society's Ohio River Museum.

First day issue of cover commemorating
150th Anniversary of State of Louisiana.